A ROOM with a ZOO

A ROOM
with a ZOO

JULES FEIFFER

Michael di Capua Books
Hyperion Books for Children

For Julie

and her family

A ROOM with a ZOO

CHAPTER 1

I have a zoo in my room. I need it. Because I'm either going to be a vet when I grow up or a zookeeper.

My father and mother and sister know I love animals. Even before I had my first, we were watching TV in my parents' bedroom and a commercial came on for dog food. I said, "I want a dog." I knew they'd say no.

And my father said, "No. You can't have a dog because you're too young to walk a dog and your mother doesn't like dogs and your sister is sixteen and she's got school and acting classes after school so she's not going to have time, so who do you think is going to end up walking your dog?"

. And I said, "You." And he said, "No, and this is why not. I've owned two dogs and walked them all hours of the day and night and I'm too old to do that ever again all by myself. You can have a dog when you're old enough to walk your dog by yourself. And sometimes I'll walk him with you."

"How old do you have to be?" I asked.

"Twelve," my father said.

"Eleven," my mother said.

"Eleven and a half," my father said.

"Ten," I said.

"Eleven," my father said.

"Ten and a half," my mother said.

That's when I got my good idea. "You don't have to walk a cat, do you?"

I could tell how really good the idea was by the expression on their faces. I could have counted up to a hundred before they said anything.

It was my mother first. "I don't see how we can get out of this."

My father said, "I think we've been tricked."

So we agreed on a cat.

CHAPTER 2

The cat was called Timmy. We got him from an animal shelter. He was just a kitten. And he had a cold. And he wouldn't eat or drink anything, and he just lay there not moving at all.

His color was like a tiger but without the stripes. Though you could see on his fur or coat where stripes should have been but they weren't. His hair was short and spiky and when I petted him, it was like I stroked straw.

I held him in my arms and in my lap. I wanted to keep him on my pillow when I went to bed, but my mother and father wouldn't let me because they were afraid I'd wake up and he'd be dead.

The first two days my father was on the phone to the animal shelter maybe ten times. Every time he hung up, he looked sadder. "What did they say?" me or my mother would ask, and every time my father gave the same answer, "They said, 'No problem.'" As if "No problem" was a kind of evil curse—like Timmy was as good as dead. It made me want to cry.

My mother hugged me and got mad at my father. She said to me, "The cat will be fine, I promise." I could tell from the 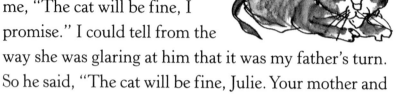 way she was glaring at him that it was my father's turn. So he said, "The cat will be fine, Julie. Your mother and I promise."

I knew he didn't believe it. But Timmy was my first and my one and only pet, so I also knew they couldn't let him die.

My father and mother and even my sister Halley took turns feeding Timmy with an eyedropper. He hardly moved. All day he just lay in one spot on the rug where the sun came in the window in the morning. My mother was nervous about a sick cat pooping in the wrong place, so wherever Timmy was lying she'd go get the litter box and put it next to him and point to it and smile. "See, Timmy? Good Timmy."

I didn't mind where he pooped, I just wanted him to get better.

It took two weeks and three visits to the vet. My father had to shove pills down his throat. Timmy spit them up. My father shoved the pill down again, and he'd hold Timmy's mouth shut tight like the vet told him. He'd stroke Timmy's throat like the vet told him. My mother and Halley and I stood around and said, "Good Timmy." It didn't matter. Timmy spit up all the pills. It was as if he didn't care if he got better or not. Only we did.

My mother and Halley, even if they didn't like animals so much, kept saying in this fake way, "I think he looks better, don't you think so?"

And when they didn't say it, I did. We hoped that saying the lie would make it come true.

And one morning I woke up and I found Timmy, looking twice as big as yesterday, scratching to pieces one of the legs of the couch which my mother got when we moved in, before I was alive. Another couch leg was already in shreds.

My mother started crying. "I'll kill that cat!" she said. But the rest of us were happy, with me the happiest.

CHAPTER 3

Maybe because he was so sick when we got him, Timmy was a scaredy-cat. He didn't let me pet him. He'd see me coming and sneak off in the other direction, which wasn't at all the way he was when he was sick. Then he always let me pick him up. I'd lay him down in my lap and he wouldn't mind staying all day, and all night too if I didn't have to get up to eat or go to the bathroom.

But now that he was all better I had to go hunt him down. It was so unfair. I'd walk into my bedroom and see his tail vanish under my bed, like he couldn't get away fast enough. So I'd crawl under the bed after him saying, "Come here, Timmy" in a very friendly and kind voice, so he'd know that the last thing I wanted to do was hurt him.

But the way he backed off from me, making himself small and flat in the shadows against the wall under my bed, it was as if I was a criminal who went around killing cats. That's how this cat who was my pet treated me. Even though I nursed him when he was sick. He could have been dead, but did he even think of that?

"Come here, Timmy," I'd say in every pleasant way that I knew how. And it didn't matter to him. He looked at me like he wanted to scream, "Here comes the cat murderer!" His eyes bugged out, his whole body curled up like this: ∩. And if he didn't run away, he made as if he was going to claw me. I reached out to him anyway to pet him. He cringed almost like my hand was a shotgun.

He wasn't always bad to me. Sometimes if I was doing something, looking at a book or I don't know what, playing with my Barbies, and my mind was a million miles away, I would look up and there he was— sitting so close I was surprised, staring right at me. And if I didn't move or do a thing, he went on staring as if we were almost friends. But if I said, "Hello, Timmy, how are you, I love you," his eyes looked at me like he was thinking, "Call the police!" And if I got up to pet him, he'd be out of there so fast I could tell he was thinking, "She's going to kill me! Dial 911!"

"I don't want this cat," I said to my mother.

"You asked for a cat, now you've got one and you don't want it," she said, as if Timmy was my fault.

"I didn't ask you to get me a cat who hates me. I hate him too."

"No, you don't," said my father, who thinks he knows what I think better than I do. "Timmy has to get used to you. You have to learn to be patient."

"Why should I learn to be patient for a cat who hates me? He should like me, because otherwise why have a pet? Nobody gets a pet because you hope someday he'll get used to you and like you. I want a nice pet. Or a dog."

So because they felt bad for me, and they weren't getting me a dog, my father took me to the pet store three blocks away to look for a make-up pet. We got a hamster.

CHAPTER 4

Who knew a hamster would be such a complicated animal to buy? Before my father let me get mine, he made me wait while he looked over the entire pet store for anything that had to do with hamsters. Different cages and tanks and water bottles and what to feed them and wheels and soft stuff for a bed like wood chips but not sawdust because it's not good for a hamster's breathing, the pet store man told us. My father didn't ask him why, so he didn't say. I wanted to ask him, but out of the house I'm very shy.

That must have been the only question my father didn't ask, but it could have been worse. It could have been my mother. When my father asks a question, he waits for an answer and then he's satisfied. Sometimes, though, he has to ask the question again because he forgets the answer the minute he hears it, not all the time but sometimes. But my mother asks questions more like it's a conversation with her best friend, with the actual question maybe five minutes later at the end. Then she has a whole other conversation about the answer. So it could be nighttime before we're out of the store.

I was getting impatient. I tugged at my father's coat to remind him that it was time to make our pick and go home. I could have been playing with my hamster for an hour by now except for my father's questions. I nudged him, and poked him, but I couldn't get him to move.

He said, "We have to prepare for the hamster's arrival the way we prepared for yours. Do you think when you were a baby we brought you home to an apartment without a crib?"

"My hamster's going to sleep in a crib?"

"Don't be a wiseguy," my father said.

Because we made such a bad mistake getting Timmy with a cold, I made sure when I looked over the hamsters that the one I picked wasn't sneezing or sniffling or the slightest bit coldy. Also I made sure *not* to get a hamster lying way back in the cage full of hamsters like he was afraid of me. Timmy taught me a good lesson about pets not to get. You look for the opposite of pets like Timmy—a perky and friendly hamster who comes to you and cuddles with you and lets you hold him in your hand, and doesn't look like he wants to call the police.

The hamster I got was very furry, small, and a light brown, kind of tan almost. He wasn't shy with me at all, which is one reason I wanted him, but the other reason was he had this look, as if all he wanted most in the world was for some kid to love him.

I was that kid. I was lucky. I named him Hammy.

"That's a terrible name," Halley said when I brought him home. But then she started calling him by his name right away. "Hello, Hammy." "Are you happy to be in our home?" "You're going to be very happy here, Hammy."

CHAPTER 5

"Why are you putting his cage up so high?" I asked my father, who was clearing my picture books off a shelf in the bookcase by the radiator in my room. It was the second shelf from the top, where I would have to stand on a chair to play with Hammy.

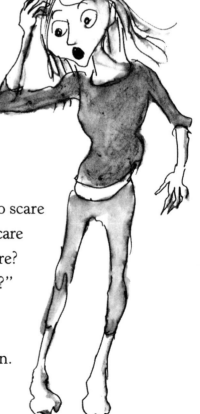

"I don't want him scared by the cat."

"Timmy will be the one who's scared," I said.

"Julie, Hammy is a rodent. He's like a mouse."

I thought he was saying that to scare me. Sometimes he says things to scare me. Anyhow, how could he be sure?

"Maybe they could be friends?"

"Are you out of your mind?" Halley said. But she always says that to me, so I didn't pay attention.

"I see cats and dogs who are friends, so why can't a cat make friends with a hamster? What if I put my hamster and my cat together and they learned to be friends, wouldn't that be a good thing to try? Especially if I'm going to be a vet?"

At last Hammy was up on his bookshelf in his very own cage, hiding out in his little plastic house with a peephole that he was too scared to peep out of. But that didn't last long—I think he was waiting for us to be alone. Because as soon as my mother and father and Halley had come and gone, which only took maybe three or four minutes, he peeked out at me from his cubbyhole. I was standing on a chair, waiting for him with a piece of lettuce. "Hello, Hammy," I said. He peeked out a little bit more, and then some more, and I could tell from the look in his eyes that he was trying to make up his mind, in or out. So I said maybe ten times, "Nice Hammy, have some lettuce, Hammy." I said it especially quiet, not to shock him because he was so small. And I thought my voice ought to be extra high like I was a really little kid until he got used to me.

So soon, very soon, he was completely out of his hole, his furry body shivering like he had a hundred little muscles pounding away inside it. But not because he was afraid, just that he was nervous in his new home. I could tell by the way he came up to me, when I was poking the lettuce at him through the wires of the cage.

He did it without a one-step-back-and-forth thing, as if he liked me. He came at me an inch at a time. I think he wanted to get to know me better. For a second or two he didn't even bother with the lettuce in my hand. Then he started nibbling. I was excited.

And who should show up to join our party? Timmy. I looked around the room for no reason, and there he was, practically six inches away, staring up at Hammy in his cage. I said, "Timmy, meet your new friend Hammy. You're going to live together so you can't eat him, okay?" I didn't expect Timmy to understand. I knew if I took Hammy out, then and there, Timmy would try to eat him. I'm not stupid.

But I was sure that with the experiment I was going to begin—this Great Experiment of mine—that after Timmy got used to Hammy, after I trained him, he would see how adorable and playful and like a little kitten he was, like a little Timmy himself, if he hadn't been so sick when we first got him.

I told my sister about my Great Experiment. "You are out of your mind" was what she said to me, but since that's what she always says, I didn't even listen. She sounded exactly the same as my mother and father warning me that Hammy was a mouse as far as Timmy goes. Except that also didn't bother me, because grown-ups know lots of old stuff they call "experience," and they think that makes them right all the time. But they can be wrong. Like my mother and father are always apologizing. "I'm sorry," he says. "No, I'm sorry," she says. So if they keep saying they're sorry, it proves they know they can be wrong. So why can't they be wrong about my Great Experiment, making Timmy and Hammy best friends?

CHAPTER 6

My best friend—actually one of my three best friends—came for an after-school play date to see my cat and hamster. Natasha's adopted like me, but not like I am, from Mount Juliet, Tennessee. She's from Russia. She was a year old when her parents went over to get her, so she doesn't have an accent. And the next year they got divorced, Natasha thinks it was over her. Her mother says no, but I think she's right because her father didn't get divorced over her two older brothers, but a year after they got her he moved out. She stays with him every other weekend, though it's more the babysitter she hangs out with.

Natasha's the smartest kid in our grade and she shows off, kind of. I only mind it a little because I learn from her, even more than from my parents. She knows stuff that grown-ups don't think of that kids want to learn.

Natasha's mother won't let her have pets because she had a guinea pig once and it died after a week.

Natasha's mother said she had enough problems with no husband and three children without taking on the extra problem of a pet who you didn't know from day to day if it was going to live or die. So Natasha likes to have play dates with friends whose parents let them have pets. Then she goes home and tells her mother about it, and that way someday she maybe can persuade her mother to buy her a parakeet, which is what she wants.

Natasha wants a parakeet as much as I want a dog. She's an expert on parakeets. She said they live seven or eight years, but some live as old as twenty. A healthy parakeet has smooth, kind of shiny feathers and the way you can tell if he's sick is if his feathers are puffed up. And the way you can tell if he's healthy is if he's playing and fussing with his feathers.

My father and mother don't know any of this stuff.

Boy parakeets have blue or bluish skin up by their nostrils, but a girl's skin is more brownish, at least that's what Natasha said. Parakeets like to trim their beaks by chewing on their perches, so you have to make sure they have wood and not plastic perches. Natasha said she was going to make her own perch when her mother lets her get a parakeet. She was going to carve it herself from an apple tree that isn't sprayed with chemicals. But she didn't tell me how she'd know whether it's sprayed or not. I wouldn't know. I'm not sure I'd recognize an apple tree if apples weren't falling off it.

Maybe because Natasha knew more about a parakeet she didn't have than I knew about the animals living in my own house, in my own room, was why I told her about my Great Experiment. It made me feel stupid, as if her imaginary parakeet was more special than Timmy and Hammy, who I had the bad luck to own. The way she made me feel, I was ready to trade Timmy and Hammy for her parakeet, even if it wasn't for real. But telling her about the Great Experiment would make us even, because it was my invention, like hers was the parakeet.

CHAPTER 7

Natasha, who knew more about pets, a lot more, than my parents or Halley, couldn't find a single reason why it shouldn't work. "But only if we do it right," she said. Whatever she meant by that, I felt too shy to ask. I was sure she'd tell me.

"Has anyone ever tried it?" she asked me.

I didn't know.

"You didn't ask at the pet store?"

I shrugged.

"Did you look in the *Guinness Book of World Records?*"

I was feeling stupid, the way Natasha did to me lots of times without even trying. But I could tell she was excited by my Great Experiment—I was glad *someone* was—and she was getting more excited by the minute. She hugged me. "Let's do it!" she whispered in my ear, though the only ones able to hear were Timmy and Hammy, who didn't understand.

Or did they? As soon as Natasha said "Let's do it!" Timmy hunched himself up like he was ready to leap.

And Hammy started racing a mile a minute round and round on his wheel. This worried me. Maybe they didn't know English, but they felt something.

"First we have to make both of them feel safe, to prove that no one wants to hurt them," Natasha said.

That would have made sense to me, except how could Timmy think Hammy could hurt him? I didn't say anything, Natasha was the boss. I was really glad the Great Experiment had a boss who wasn't me. I'm good at getting ideas, but I'm not good after that, so I did everything Natasha told me.

I slipped Hammy out of his cage. His heart was beating like crazy because he could smell Timmy even when he couldn't see him. Timmy was leaning forward, his neck pushed out like it was trying to leave his body, his head pointed straight at Hammy, his whiskers stuck out like arrows. I never saw him do that before.

Suddenly Natasha leaned over and scooped him up in her arms. She pressed her face into his fur. "Nice Timmy, nice Timmy." Timmy squirmed, but she held him tighter.

"Now what?" I said, holding Hammy high over my head. My heart was beating almost as fast as his was.

"Let's try the bathtub," Natasha said.

Before I could ask why, she told me in an almost grown-up voice, sounding as important as our fourth-grade teacher, Mrs. Korman. "The bathtub will be their club. That's where they will go to meet. My father has a club he goes to. He eats lunch with me there on Saturdays. He sees the people who aren't his friends who he never sees otherwise and he would never see them except they have this club.

"When I'm big, I'll belong to his club. I'll see him there whenever we want, and after I can go to my house and he goes to his house. The club will be our special place, and that's what the bathtub is gonna be for Timmy and Hammy, their club, where everything's different. And Hammy doesn't have to be in a cage and it's safe, like the bathtub's a nest. And they start to be friends. Timmy and Hammy, it's gonna be so great!"

Natasha always changes my mind from what I'm thinking to what she's thinking, which is different from my parents or Halley, who when they're thinking one thing and I'm not, I know I'm right. I wasn't afraid of my Great Experiment anymore. I was dying to try it. Very gently I put Hammy down in the tub. He didn't look happy. He ran back and forth across the tub, he jumped and fell back in and then ran back and forth

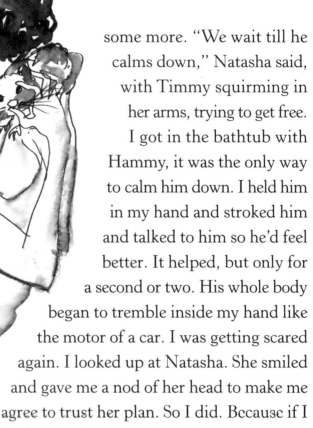

some more. "We wait till he calms down," Natasha said, with Timmy squirming in her arms, trying to get free. I got in the bathtub with Hammy, it was the only way to calm him down. I held him in my hand and stroked him and talked to him so he'd feel better. It helped, but only for a second or two. His whole body began to tremble inside my hand like the motor of a car. I was getting scared again. I looked up at Natasha. She smiled and gave me a nod of her head to make me agree to trust her plan. So I did. Because if I didn't, she'd get mad at me—that's how she is—and she might not be my friend anymore.

And then—it was the last thing in the world I thought she was going to do—she dropped Timmy out of her arms and he was with us in the bathtub.

"Bad cat!" she screamed. "I'm bleeding!"

Timmy was attacking me in the bathtub, trying to get at Hammy, but the bathtub was slippery and his legs were moving too fast for him to keep his balance. He slid all over the bathtub, and the more he slid, the faster his legs went out from under him, which only made his sliding worse. I was trying to think of what to do with Hammy in my hands when suddenly he wasn't anymore. He made a leap I couldn't believe, a foot high over the top of the tub, as if he was a monkey, not a hamster.

"I'm hurt, you're not even looking!" yelled Natasha.

Timmy jumped higher even than Hammy, who was running around in circles because the bathroom door was closed and he couldn't get out. I grabbed for Timmy from where I was sitting in the bathtub. I caught him by the back leg in midair, which drove him crazy. He turned on me with his teeth fanged like a tiger in the jungle. I had to let go or he'd bite me.

"I'm bleeding, I'm wounded!" Natasha wanted to get my attention, but I didn't have time. Maybe Timmy did bite her, but it looked more like a scratch to me— okay, a long scratch. It made her not care about my Great Experiment anymore. She just wanted out of the bathroom.

She punched the door with her fist. The door flew open and Hammy was a mile-a-minute out of there, and Timmy too, running even with Natasha. She tripped over him and fell, with Timmy tangled between her legs, twisting like a tornado not to get squished. By the time he was on his feet again, he didn't know which way he was going.

Where my mother was, in the kitchen, I heard screams. Coming out of the kitchen, right at me, was

Hammy. What a dumb thing to do because Timmy was waiting behind me. "Hammy, NO!" I yelled at the top of my lungs, which scared Hammy enough to turn him around, a second before Timmy would have had him. He ran back toward the kitchen with Timmy after him, practically on top of him.

Our front door, which is next to the kitchen, opened and—I couldn't believe it—the same second Halley walked in, home from her acting class, Hammy ran out. The elevator in the hall behind Halley closed, but not before Hammy got in.

Halley didn't know what was going on. Timmy and Natasha were running in a race to the front door. Natasha had her head ducked low like a football player. "I want my mother!" she screamed.

Halley hated Natasha because she thought she pushed me around, so whatever she wanted, Halley did the opposite. She slammed the front door and Natasha and Timmy crashed into it at the same time. "You hurt me!" Natasha yelled so loud I bet you could hear her on the street.

I didn't care because Hammy was saved. He went down in the elevator.

CHAPTER 8

It wasn't my fault, but you wouldn't know it from how they treated me. The important thing was Hammy was saved (he saved himself, okay?). And Timmy couldn't run without tripping over his own legs, so nothing happened. Nobody got hurt. Besides, it wasn't my idea, it was totally Natasha's, who hardly talked to me anymore. In the schoolyard she practically held her nose walking past me. I was two inches away and she didn't see me, yeah, right. She was mad at me because of her bite, which it wasn't. It was a scratch.

No matter how much I proved to my parents the whole thing was Natasha's fault, they wouldn't answer me because they couldn't because they knew I was right. They just shook their heads very slow, very very sad and slow, as if they couldn't believe their daughter would commit this terrible crime.

Okay, let them. I didn't care, or if I did, it was only a little bit, and that was because it was so unfair.

What happened, really and truly? Nothing! Hammy

came back up in the elevator when my mother pushed the button. Hiding in the corner where you couldn't even see him if you weren't looking, and so sweet when I picked him up in my hand. He rubbed his nose against my thumb. Hammy wasn't mad at me, and if anyone had the right to be . . .

If you're interested in who actually suffered— besides me!—it was poor Timmy. He hid under my bed for a whole day, not even coming out to eat. What he did about pooping and pee-pee, I don't want to know.

And when he finally came out in the middle of the next day, he just went back to lying on the rug. He might as well have been frozen or dead, the way he stared at Hammy running circles on his wheel. But it

wasn't like he wanted to eat him, but more like when there's something you really and truly want but you know you'll never get it, and you don't deserve it, and you'll die without it ever happening. So you might as well not be a cat anymore.

That stare was going to drive me crazy if I didn't do something to change it. And if the Great Experiment didn't work, it didn't mean there might not be a *Greater* Experiment that would work.

I began to have bad thoughts going into my bedroom—kind of like it was haunted. Most of the time I stayed away, bugging my mother in the dining room, which she used for an office, about my Greater Experiment and how I needed some ideas. I was waiting for the right one and maybe she had it. But her only idea was that I shouldn't talk so much. "I have to warn you, I'm running out of patience, Julie."

And Halley started standing with her body pressed against her bedroom door so I couldn't get in. "I don't know what you're talking about! Go away!"

But I wasn't going away. I couldn't. And I couldn't figure out how to help Timmy. Except by feeding him Hammy.

I had to stop worrying about it. That's all I did from the time I woke up till I went to bed at night. I didn't know what to do.

"I want a dog," I said at dinner one night. My father

groaned. It had gotten to be very sad in our house.

When I was in bed later on, I heard my mother and father in their bedroom talking in low voices, so low that I knew it was about me and they were afraid I might hear, even though I was supposed to be asleep. It made me feel a little better that they were talking about me. But then I heard them laugh. It hurt my feelings. I didn't think there was anything to laugh about.

The next afternoon I got home from school and had to go in my room. It was against my will, but I had to dump my book bag and stuff. And I found a big gray and red fish I never saw before in a huge tank of water with a filter that bubbled and pebbles and coral and grass at the bottom. And this mean-looking fish swam around like he owned the place. And Timmy was lying on my rug, staring up at it on the bookshelf, just under Hammy's cage. And he didn't look sad anymore. Just the opposite.

CHAPTER 9

Watching my fish was like watching television. I sat on the floor and it went back and forth a thousand times. I could have watched forever. Timmy too. We sat together, which never happened, even with TV. Sometimes Timmy climbed into my lap, which he hadn't done once since he was a kitten and sick.

The fish was my mother's idea—or my father's— they both said they had it. They wanted to buy a big, strange-looking fish to take Timmy's mind off Hammy to make him feel better. I don't know why they thought buying a second animal he couldn't eat would make him feel better. But so far so good.

I would have thought Timmy would go even more crazy with the two of them up there. But when my father put the new fish tank on the bookshelf, Timmy kind of forgot about Hammy. He hardly ever looked at him anymore, even though the tank was just under Hammy's cage. When he did, he got this sort of surprised look on his face like he had to remind himself,

"Hey, don't I know you from somewhere?"

My mother told me she never would have bought such a big tank and so much equipment, but since my father didn't know anything about fish, he got too much of everything.

My father wasn't sure he did the right thing either. He was worried that the fish would die any minute. Which is why he told me he filled and refilled the tank three times before I came home and put in the gravel on the bottom and took some out and put even more in and then took it all out because he forgot to wash it, like he

was supposed to, before he put it in. And then he put rocks in, which he remembered to scrub first, and he built a cave with the rocks like the instruction book on fish said to do, by putting a bunch of rocks in a circle in the middle of the tank and then you put a flat rock on top like it's a roof. Then he put in some plants with long, skinny, wavy leaves. And to make you know if the water is too warm or cold, he taped a thermometer inside the tank, and he put in a filter.

Red Tiger Oscar was the name they said in the pet store that my fish was. I called him Oscar. Oscar was six or eight inches long and wide and flat and dangerous-looking. His dark gray color made him look like a gangster on TV. His wide body made him look like a gangster wearing an overcoat—with blood on it. Wavy speckles of dark red, kind of like dried blood, spread across the whole bottom part of his body. It was scary, but nice scary.

His eyes were black like a gangster's, and on top of his eyes there was a bright red line the color of his speckles. "He reminds me of Tony Soprano," my father said, so he called my fish Tony. He's a famous TV gangster. Oscar moved very slow across the tank like he was following somebody for revenge. Maybe another gangster who had robbed him. Timmy and I watched all day. I made up stories for Timmy to keep him from getting bored.

"Once upon a time Oscar and Hammy and Timmy were on their way to Grandma's house and they were in the woods and a wolf came up to them and he said, 'Where are you going by the hair of my chinny-chin-chin?' And they said, 'We're going to Grandma's house.' And the wolf said, 'Okay then, goodbye.' And he took a shortcut and he knocked on Grandma's door and she said, 'Who is it?' And the wolf said, 'It's Oscar and Hammy and Timmy.' So Grandma said, 'Okay, you can come in.' And so the wolf went in and he ate up Grandma. And when Oscar and Hammy and Timmy came and knocked on the door, the wolf said, 'Who's there?' And they said, 'It's Oscar and Hammy and Timmy.' And the wolf who was disguised as Grandma said, 'Come in by the hair of my chinny-chin-chin.' So they came in with an ax and chopped off the wolf's head because they knew it was the wolf because he said, 'Chinny-chin-chin.' And Grandma climbed out of the hole in the wolf's neck and she was safe and sound. And they sat down to eat the wolf for dinner. And the lesson of this story is if you eat somebody else, watch out, because somebody else will eat you."

CHAPTER 10

After a week with us, Oscar started to hide out in the little rock cave at the bottom of the tank my father made. Maybe he really was a gangster. He stayed there as much as he swam around. I missed him. So did Timmy. We sat on the floor and looked at his tank and waited and waited.

I called to him, "Oscar, Oscar." I stood on the chair I spray-painted last year but it needs another coat. I tapped my finger on the tank. "Come out, come out, wherever you are, Oscar." But he wasn't listening.

He came out only when I fed him. So I fed him more and more, dry flakes and frozen fish stuff, and he'd gulp it down like candy. And then he'd go back into his cave, which was getting too small for him.

"Tony Soprano is getting fat," my mother said.

"He's growing, and his name is Oscar."

"You're feeding him too much, honey," she said.

"You don't know, you don't even like fish."

"*Please*, Julie." She looked a little mad.

I can't help it if it's true. What was I supposed to do, lie? She can't stand fish or any pets. I don't know what she's going to do when I'm old enough to have a dog. She doesn't even know how to pet a dog. She does it the wrong way. She pets up when you're supposed to pet down.

Ste pets up when you're supposed to pet down.

So how did she know Oscar was fat? He was growing because he was big and healthy, which is what a fish is supposed to be. Lots of fish, when you bring them home, get sick and die right away. Natasha had a fish who died. And so did Melanie. And Letitia. But their fishes never looked as healthy as Oscar.

Anyway, he was less scary when he was fat. He didn't look so much like a gangster in a coat anymore, he looked cute. I'm the one with him all day, me and Timmy. So I could tell what was wrong better than my mother. Oscar was lonesome, that's all. He needed some fish to play with.

CHAPTER 11

I picked out the fish. There were three of them and they were big. Not as big as Oscar, but it was safer to have a bigger fish over a littler fish, the man in the store said, because Oscar could eat a littler fish. And actually I saw fish so little swimming around in tanks that I bet Oscar would have eaten them. So the way I picked out the fish was, I'd go from tank to tank with Halley, who took me, and we argued about it.

"He'd eat that one," Halley said.

"No, he wouldn't."

"Yes, he would."

"You're lying."

The man in the store was no help because he said Oscar could eat anything, so no fish was safe. But I didn't believe him, and Halley thought that the way the man looked at her, he didn't like her. So we made up our own minds.

We got three Fantails, which are goldfish, because they were beautiful but also big. They were almost as big as Oscar and sort of wide too. And such a gorgeous red, it was hard to believe it wasn't painted on. You could believe it in a picture or a magazine, but not in real life. I mean if it wasn't on a fish, it would look freaky. If you saw a person coming down the street and she was that red, you'd go, "No way!" I wouldn't want a dog that red. Clifford the dog is red, but not red-red. Anyhow, he's not real. Anyhow, it doesn't matter because I wouldn't buy a dog like Clifford. Mine will be a Chihuahua.

I didn't think Oscar would be such a gangster around Reddy—which is what I decided to name them, all three of my new fish. They all looked exactly the same, so why not?

When we put them in the tank, Oscar stayed hidden in his rock hole. He wouldn't even say hello, but Timmy did. He couldn't take his eyes off my three Reddys, like he was hypnotized. How could he not fall in love with fishes so red? Poor Hammy ran around like crazy on his wheel. Nobody hardly looked at him anymore.

Red wasn't my Reddys only color. They had a kind of gold middle around their bellies and a long swishy white veil at the back of their fins that you could see through, and it was so pretty the way it floated, like the train part of a wedding dress.

I said to Timmy their whole first day home, "You'll

have to be patient, Timmy, soon Oscar will come out and make friends." But he hadn't by bedtime. And the next morning when I woke up, one of the Reddys was missing.

I screamed so loud my mother and father and Halley came running in. Halley tried to calm me down. She always tries to calm me down when I'm too excited, but now I was too excited for a good reason. I kept pointing

at the tank and screaming, "Look! Look! Look!" It took a minute for them to figure it out, because what I was pointing at for them to look at wasn't there anymore.

The first thing my father did was find a big glass jar in a kitchen cabinet high up somewhere, so he had to climb on a ladder and my mother and Halley said, "Be careful," because my father doesn't have good balance. And I didn't want him to break a leg because of me and the bad thing I made happen.

And he filled the jar with water and he put the other two Reddys in. Oscar was back in his cave. Hiding. I hoped he felt bad. But if he lived to be a hundred, he couldn't feel half as bad as I did. I should have listened to the man in the store.

I felt so awful I couldn't look at my two other Reddys without crying. They reminded me too much of my missing Reddy. "Take them back to the store," I begged my father.

Oscar could stay in his cave forever. He should be in jail for the gangster he was. I thought of giving him away, to Natasha. And we could be friends again. But I couldn't give him away, because it was my fault more than his. I didn't want to have to look at him for a long, long time, especially those red speckles on his body from one end to the other. They were like the ghost of Reddy inside his tummy, shining through, reminding me of my badness.

CHAPTER 12

My mother and father couldn't, no matter how hard they tried, make me feel better over Reddy. First of all, it's a parent's job to make you feel better, so whatever they said I wasn't going to believe them. For instance, they said in a day or two I'd get over it. The more they said it, the more I knew I wouldn't.

Halley was actually the one who helped. She said, "Julie, it's my fault more than yours because I should have known better. And I did, but I let you talk me into it."

She lets me talk her into things a lot because she loves me so much. And that made me feel less bad. Then she and I played a game of Zoolionaire on her computer, and by the time I won I didn't think about Reddy so much anymore.

My father said he'd take Oscar back to the store and exchange him for more Reddys, or any other kind of fish who wouldn't eat each other. The second I said "That's a good idea," I felt sad. I didn't ever want to see

Oscar again, but I couldn't tell my father right that minute I never wanted to see him again. In a couple of days, maybe.

Except in a couple of days I was back to liking Oscar. The more I thought about it, the whole thing was my fault. The man at the store warned me that Oscar was going to eat any fish he felt like. I should have listened. If I got rid of Oscar, then maybe I should be gotten rid of too. Since my parents would never do that and I was kind of Oscar's parent, how could I do it to him? You have to keep your child even when he's bad. So I had to keep Oscar and make myself forgive him.

CHAPTER 13

What made everything better was the turtle my mother got for me. She said it was the kind of pet she could appreciate. It didn't do anything. It just sat on a rock in its tank most of the time looking out at the wall.

She got the idea, she said, having lunch with her girlfriend Martha, who she told about my fish and how sad I was. And Martha said, "She needs a new pet." And they spent the rest of the lunch talking about what kind.

And no matter what Martha said—

"Bird . . ."

"Rabbit . . ."

"Snake . . ."

"Lizard . . ."

—my mother went, "Yich."

Until Martha said, "How about a turtle? Do you hate turtles?"

And my mother said, "I don't think I hate them." And she thought about it and decided she didn't. Or if she did, not that much.

So on the way home, she went to our pet store and asked the man who Halley says doesn't like her about turtles. I guess because she decided to give him a second chance. Besides, the way my mother makes everything into a conversation, everybody likes her. They had this long talk about how he lived in New Jersey and his mother didn't want him coming to work in New York City every day, so he was thinking of quitting the pet store and going back to school in New Jersey to be a science teacher. So even if he sold us the wrong fish last time because he hated Halley, he wouldn't do that to my mother because she made him her friend.

Turtelini looked like a midget dinosaur stuck inside a rock. He had these little black eyes that I don't know where they were looking, never at me. And the kind of expression that made me wonder the way I never I did with Timmy or Hammy or Oscar whether or not he had feelings.

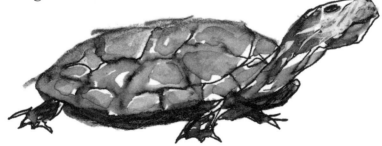

He had this red stripe on both sides of his head where his ears should have been, but I couldn't see them, if he had them. To me he looked really smart, but what could he be smart about if he lived his whole life inside a tank? When he moved, it was hardly at all. Mostly he creeped underwater onto a small pile of rocks my father put in a corner of his tank. He climbed on top every day out of the water, and sat there until it was dark, with his neck sticking way out of his shell like a fat noodle.

Sometimes he stood up against the glass and scratched hard with his claws like he was trying to break out. But he didn't do that a lot or I would have worried. When I went near him, he stuck his head back inside his shell and it took a long time for him to come out again. I wanted him to like me, but I don't think he did.

My mother called him "Shy One." My father called him "Rocky." Only Halley called him by his right name. My parents thought it was funny to give my pets joke names, but it was the opposite of funny. It hurt my feelings. First, they bought me these animals and then they made fun of them. I mean, if my mother's going to make fun of my turtle, why did she buy him for me in the first place? Or why did my father change the water in his tank every two days and scrub the rocks he found in Riverside Park for him to climb out of the water on?

CHAPTER 14

Mrs. Korman, my fourth-grade teacher, gave us the best homework in my life. It was as if I made up the assignment myself. That's how good it was.

The homework was to pick your favorite animal. And write a composition as if you're that animal, and tell why you'd rather be it than anyone else. Also, you're supposed to do research, and you have to write a whole page and not just a couple of sentences, which is what a lot of our class would do if you let them. Me too, but not if I can write about animals.

The title was my father's idea. But the rest I made up myself.

I, CHIHUAHUA

I am a dog named Chihuahua. I am the smallest breed of dog there is. You can carry me around in a backpack or a tote bag or even a purse. I don't care. I like it. I go on trips on planes and trains. Bigger dogs can't. That's one thing that makes me glad I'm a Chihuahua.

I come from Mexico originally. But now I'm popular all over the world. That's because I'm good with people. I'm good with pets. Even some cats.

I love people, but I love my master the most. She is the one who picked me out. Before I belonged to anybody, she saw me, and out of all the dogs in the kennel, I was the one she wanted. She feeds me and grooms me. Once a week she brushes my teeth with a little toothbrush. She lets me sleep on her bed anytime I want.

I don't like cold weather. That's because I came from Mexico originally. It's hotter there than New York.

I am definitely not an outdoor dog. I am a lapdog. But don't think I don't like to run around. I have lots of energy. The way I use up all my energy is I run from room to room in our apartment. It is best for a Chihuahua like me to live in a big apartment. Or a house.

The last thing I want to tell you about is that my body is only a little bit longer than my tail. My hair feels smooth when you stroke it. It is short.

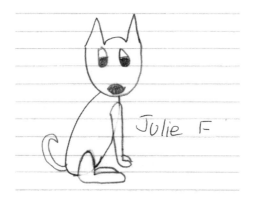

CHAPTER 15

My parents have a friend named Judith who, when she comes over for coffee, brings her dog Sophie sometimes. Sophie is as big as me almost, and she's an Airedale, and she's gray and white and acts like a puppy though she's five. I mean, she's not too trained. And her hair is short, and when I stroke her, it stings a little.

But it's not polite to talk about the dog before I talk about Judith, this friend of my parents. My mother would call that bad manners. Actually, Sophie is the one I'm interested in, but I'll have good manners and tell about Judith, even if it's kind of boring.

Judith is very pretty, blah-blah, with springy, bushy black hair, like mine is sometimes, and she's not married and she's a writer like my mother and father. But my father does other things, I don't know if Judith does. My mother also does stand-up comedy. I think maybe everybody who works at home and not in an office does more things than people who just go to work in an office, because they don't have to get on a subway and go home. They're home already so they have all this extra time.

Judith talks almost as much as my mother and they like to talk at the same time. So I don't know how they know who's saying what, but they do and they laugh at it. They laugh at stuff I don't get. And this happens every time—Judith, when she laughs, forgets she has to hold on to Sophie. And she drops the leash and Sophie runs like a crazy dog through the whole apartment—we have nine rooms—barking. My mother hates Sophie.

So Judith starts running after Sophie. Through every room she yells, "No, Sophie, bad Sophie, come, Sophie!" But she says it in such a nicey-nice voice that Sophie can tell Judith isn't really mad at her, she's kidding. So Sophie does it some more, the running through the whole apartment.

Timmy disappears when Sophie comes over. I don't know where he goes. But Hammy and Turtelini don't care. I don't think they know about dogs, like that they even exist. They could even think all that barking is thunder.

Judith doesn't catch Sophie until Sophie lets her. And then she hugs her with both her arms and Sophie tries to get away again, and sometimes Judith can't hold her because of how big and strong she is. Judith is bigger, but I don't think she's as strong. And Sophie runs back to the front of the apartment, where my mother is sitting in the kitchen with a cigarette she said she was just going to hold in her fingers but not smoke. And she's smoking it because Sophie makes her smoke.

Sophie and Judith aren't helping me get my dog. I know what my mother is thinking at the kitchen table, smoking a cigarette that's Sophie's fault. It's about me getting a dog, and she's thinking, "Over my dead body."

CHAPTER 16

Two weeks before spring vacation, Mrs. Korman put up a Butch Bide-A-Wee sheet on the class bulletin board, and I made sure my name was at the top, even though I had to be a pest to do it. I didn't care, it was too important.

Okay, I did care a little. And Mrs. Korman hurt my feelings every time she said in front of the class, "Julie, I wish you'd stop asking when the Butch sheet is going up. All in good time."

She had to know how much it meant to me because I told her at least ten times that I needed to take Butch, who's our class rabbit, home for spring break. Butch lives in a big cage in the back of the classroom in a kind of make-believe forest. Or that's what it's supposed to be, but it looks sort of dumb. I mean, some fake grass and a couple of rocks and a couple of plants, but they're in little plastic boxes, and some paper daisies. The only cool thing about it is the stream Mrs. Korman made by hanging a water bottle on the cage that drips very slowly into a plastic pan that covers the front part of the cage that's covered with dirt, so when enough water drips in, it looks like a creek or a spring.

But you have to make sure it doesn't overflow. So every hour or so, some kid has to volunteer to empty the pan, which is full or almost full by then, and put it back to fill up again with water. And then you have to fill the water bottle to the top so it can start dripping again into the creek, which Butch the rabbit is supposed to drink out of, but he never does. He drinks right off the bottom of the long tube that drips the water into the pan.

I'm the volunteer who fills the water bottle and empties the pan more than anyone else, so it's only right that my name should be at the top of the Butch Bide-A-Wee list. I had the most experience emptying the pan and filling the bottle.

Jenna said she did it as much as me, but she's lying. I got scared that Mrs. Korman wouldn't know the truth, because Jenna put her name second on the list and then started talking about how excited her mother and father were that Butch might go to their house, and they were already fixing it up to make it safe for him.

Then Gabriella put her name down third and said her family was going to vacation in the country and they would take Butch with them and leave him outside in the garden in his cage so he could enjoy the outdoors, and that her mother and father couldn't wait for their adventure to begin.

The rest of the names on the list didn't bother me. They were kids who put their name on every list just to show off, but you know they'll make up a reason to back out at the last minute.

But Jenna and Gabriella worried me. I didn't know why they were doing this to me, they were supposed to be my friends. What worried me most was all this talk about how their parents couldn't wait. Because I had a feeling my parents couldn't wait for Butch *not* to come home. It was such a strong feeling that even though it was Mrs. Korman's rule that your name couldn't go on the list until you brought in a letter from your parents saying it was okay, I put my name down anyway. I promised Mrs. Korman I'd bring in my letter tomorrow.

I meant to. I tried. I kept trying and kept not asking. For example, I tried to ask—not my father, more my mother—but it wasn't a good time. Some days, if I wanted to ask her something, she'd say, "Julie, this isn't a good time." And now it was like that every day.

For two weeks after the Butch list went up, whenever I thought it was maybe all right to ask, I'd go to her and I knew right away that it was going to be "Julie, this isn't a good time." I can tell that look a mile away. I knew it was getting way late to ask. It was wrong not to ask. But some things you do wrong aren't really your fault, and this was one of them. And that's why Jenna and Gabriella had permission and not me.

And then it was four days before vacation and Mrs. Korman told the class, "Tomorrow we put the names in a hat of whoever's on the list who wants Butch for spring vacation, and we pick the winner, but if you haven't got a letter from your parents saying you have permission, then we take your name off the list."

By that time, I wanted Butch more than anything in my whole life. But I knew my mother wasn't going to give me permission. She might have two weeks ago when the list went up, but now it was too late. Why didn't I ask right away, when the list went up? It worried me that I kept meaning to ask and I didn't. And it was going to worry me until I gave myself a really good reason for not asking. But the way I was feeling, I didn't think that was ever going to happen.

Then it happened. I was feeding my animals which I do first thing, every day when I get home after school. First, I feed Hammy his pellets, then I feed Oscar his flakes, then I feed Turtelini his nuggets. Timmy walks an inch behind me all the time, sometimes closer. He rubs his side against my leg, he rubs his nose on me, his jaw, the top of his head, and every other part of his body that he can rub, he rubs against my leg. Until I'm ready to feed him. Timmy's always last.

I finished with Hammy and Turtelini and Oscar, and then I opened a can of wet cat food. I took a fork and I scooped the cat food into Timmy's bowl. I wasn't even thinking about it. I was only trying to get the goopy part of the cat food off the fork where it was stuck and into Timmy's bowl. I was sorry for poor Timmy, who was running around me and past me and right at me and back and forth like a crazy cat, like he hadn't been fed in a week. And that's when I knew why I couldn't ask my mother for permission to bring Butch home for spring vacation. The reason was the dog.

I wanted a dog. I wanted a dog so badly I was scared to ask for something I also wanted a lot but not as badly as I wanted a dog. Because what if I used up all my asks? The dog was my main ask, he was my ask number 1. And if I made Butch the rabbit my first ask, before my ask number 1, my mother and father could say that it was one ask too many.

I didn't think they'd be mean like that after they said I could maybe have a dog when I got to be ten and a half. But that was before I asked for Butch, so they could say, "Well, we didn't know about the rabbit when you asked for the dog, so that changes everything." I couldn't take a chance, I was too scared.

That very afternoon Mrs. Korman told me she couldn't wait anymore for me to bring a note signed by my parents. What was I supposed to do? I went home after school and I finally asked. And I was right to be worried. My mother got angry: "Now you ask to bring a rabbit home in two days for two weeks? Julie, what was on your mind, didn't you think?"

The question was so unfair it made me cry. No matter how many times I explained, "It's not my fault," my mother couldn't understand. The more she couldn't understand, the more upset she got, which made me cry even harder. She tried to calm us both down. "I'll talk to your father tonight and see if we can work this out," she said. "But tomorrow I'm going to complain to Mrs. Korman for letting this wait so long. I am going to bawl her out."

And that's what made me fall on the floor screaming "No!" Which changed my mother's mind about saying anything to Mrs. Korman.

CHAPTER 17

I held the note in my hand. Written by my mother and signed by her, and this is what it said, I memorized it word for word. "Dear Mrs. Korman, This is to inform you that Julie has our permission to board Butch the rabbit in our apartment during the spring break. We will be happy to pick him up and whatever else goes with him. We hope Julie turns out to be the lucky girl, but our good wishes to the winner of the Butch competition. Sincerely," and she signed both their names, not just Jenny Feiffer but Jules Feiffer too, so that Mrs. Korman knew that my permission letter had both my parents' names on it and Jenna and Gabriella had only one. I know, because they showed me. Jenna had her mother's, Gabriella had her father's. But I had both. Which proved that my parents were involved. Which is what my school wants parents to be. *My* parents would be around for Butch a lot more than Jenna's and Gabriella's. Unless they were very busy. And then they would have to be very, very, extra busy.

I put the note in my book bag and then I thought it might get lost in my book bag, so I put it in my coat pocket, but then I got scared it would get crushed in my pocket, so I carried it in my hand, but then I was afraid I might drop it if I tripped in the street and it could get run over by a car. So I put it back in my book bag, where I checked on it every block to make sure it hadn't fallen out, and since I didn't think the place I put it, next to my notebook, was safe enough, I found a safer place, and then an even safer place, and finally I found a secret place where Jenna and Gabriella would never think of looking if they were trying to steal it, which was on my mind that they might try, though I knew they wouldn't. But you can't be too safe. And anyhow, what if I got robbed? In my secret place, they'd never find the note.

Mrs. Korman called it the Butch lottery. She was going to put our three names down on little scraps of paper and mix them up in a hat and ask for a volunteer, and the volunteer was going to pick the winner, and it better be me. But the closer it came to happening, I knew it wasn't going to be. I just felt it, like I had seen it happen already like a movie in my head. I saw the hand pick out the winner's name on the scrap of paper. And the winner was JENNA! Or the winner was GABRIELLA! I never saw in my head that the winner was Julie.

"Do you have the note from your parents, Julie?" Mrs. Korman asked first thing as I got to my desk. And though it didn't matter anymore because I wasn't going to win, I said, "Yes," and she said, "Where is it?" And I unzipped my book bag to give it to her, and it was exactly what I was afraid of. Somebody stole it.

I looked in every inch of my book bag. I said, "I have it here, it's in here, Mrs. Korman."

She said, "Just take your time, you'll find it." But she was lying. I took my time and didn't find it. I emptied my book bag—all of it. On my desk. I opened up every book, my notebook that I remembered hiding it next to, but it wasn't there, my social-studies book, my library book. It wasn't anywhere! How could that be? It was gone! It was impossible!

I was this close—I mean it—this close to crying, when—duh—I remembered my secret place.

I had forgotten all about my secret place. I don't know why, maybe because I thought of all the other places first, which made me forget my secret place. Nobody stole my note. It was in my secret place, my darling, lovely secret place.

My secret place wasn't where it should have been. I looked twenty times, and everywhere I looked, it didn't have a secret place. I felt around in my book bag like crazy. All that was left was my letter somewhere, in my secret place somewhere. My hands went over every inch feeling for a lump an envelope with a letter in it might make, a tiny little lump that would say to me, "You dummy, I'm right here. You don't have to cry."

Mrs. Korman said, "Julie, I'm very sorry, but we can't wait."

"Can't we pick tomorrow? I'll get another note!"

"Julie," Mrs. Korman said in a soft voice, like if she said my name as if she liked me, whatever she said after I shouldn't feel as miserable as I already did. Because this was the worst thing that ever happened to me. Because I was the one who was going to be picked! The volunteer was going to reach into the hat and pick out

JULIE! Me! I absolutely knew it!

Except my name wasn't in the hat. Because I didn't have a note. But I did have a note. It was there in the classroom, in my secret place. Why couldn't Mrs. Korman understand?

Everything that happened afterwards was unfair. Joel was the volunteer Mrs. Korman picked, but it was a mistake, because he always made fun of me and called me Ghoulie when my name is Julie. So he was an unfair volunteer to pick. And then he picked Jenna's name out of the hat when it was unfair to have any names in the hat if mine wasn't going to be there. And everybody clapped when Jenna's name was announced, so I had to show I was a good sport because that's what my mother says I have to be when it's not fair. So I clapped so loud everybody looked at me like, Why is she clapping so loud? So even when I'm a good sport, it's not fair. Starting with the note, it was the most unfair day of my life.

CHAPTER 18

The last thing I wanted to do with Butch stolen from me was ballroom dancing. But the morning before spring break my whole grade had to go onstage in the auditorium and do an exhibition. Also, parents were invited.

Up until Butch, I thought it was going to be fun. But now nothing was fun and wouldn't be for a long time, if ever. And I was hoping I would wake up sick and get out of it, but I didn't.

My class had been rehearsing twice a week all term with all the other fourth-grade classes. A substitute who danced in a movie once came from outside Tuesdays and Thursdays to teach us. Her name was Maeve. She was like a stage actress and talked slow and very loud, as if she was in a play. And whatever she said, it was like she memorized it before she said it and then said it because it was her part. If she was mad at us for moving around when she'd told us twice to stand still, she said: "When—I—tell—you—to—

stand—still—and—be—silent—what—part—of—that—do—you—not—understand?"

It was almost as if she was kidding, it sounded so fake. Except she meant it. You could tell from her eyes and the way she didn't smile. The funny part was, the more serious Maeve got, the more actressy it sounded. I don't mean that in a bad way. I liked her. She had curly gray hair. She was old, maybe fifty, and tall and skinny. So when she walked, which was kind of funny, with her feet pointing out, she looked like a boy. After every rehearsal, we took turns imitating her. That was almost as much fun as the dancing.

Everybody had a dance partner. Mine was Joseph, whose family came from Ecuador, but he was born here. He's very polite— or maybe shy—and doesn't talk much to girls. But I watched him in the yard talking a mile a minute to his friends, who are all boys, and even if he doesn't have an Ecuador accent I couldn't understand a word he said because he talked too fast and laughed so hard.

But with me he didn't laugh. He stood extra straight when we danced the fox-trot, which is forward, forward, slide, together, forward, forward, slide, together. Maeve shouted at us, in this extra-loud voice she used as if she wasn't standing a foot away from us. "You—are—not—in—thee—United—States—Marines—Joseph. You—are—not—marching—off—to—war. You—are—do—ing—thee—fox—trot—Julie—stop—giggling—and—pay—attention—to—your—feet."

Which only made Joseph more shy, so he stood stiffer. I knew the only reason Maeve picked on me was to make Joseph think she wasn't only picking on him. But I didn't care, I'm a good dancer. Everyone says so, and if it made Joseph feel better for me to be picked on, I didn't mind.

Three days before spring break, the day before they gave my rabbit away, Maeve was extra high-strung, even for an actress, maybe because we were going to

dance this song, "Lullaby of Broadway," in front of all these kids and parents and the principal, and we rehearsed and rehearsed it, and we still couldn't stay in step. After all those weeks, the way it looked was like a bunch of kids fooling around, some of us dancing it right and some of us couldn't get in step and some of us faking it. So Maeve was really upset, and she yelled in her loudest, fakiest voice, "I—do—not—have—to—be—doing—this. I—have—studied—acting—with (some name I never heard of)—and—I—have—studied—dance—with—Twilla (or some name like that I never heard of)—so—I—do—not—have—to—teach—you—ballroom—dancing—if—you—do—not—want—to—learn—ballroom—dancing—because—you—are—savages. Well—what—are—you? Ballroom—dancers—or—are—you—savages?"

And Joseph was the first. He started to wave his

arms up and down in the air like crazy, and he went, "Ooga Booga, Ooga Booga." He started jumping up and down like he was a savage. I mean, that wasn't like him. And then a couple of his friends decided that they had to do it too, it looked like so much fun. They started jumping around, going "Ooga Booga, Ooga Booga."

The rest of us didn't do anything. We were too scared. What Maeve did was walk out of the classroom. Which was the worst thing she could have done, it made us feel so ashamed. So when she came back maybe three minutes later and all she said was "One—more—time" and she put on the record of "Lullaby of Broadway," we did it better and more in step than ever before. When the lesson was over, even though Maeve left the room without saying a word, I knew we had done it right for the first time.

And the only time. We rehearsed the next to last day before spring break and it was as bad as always. Or just a little better, but not enough to make Maeve talk to us again. She had hardly said two words to us since the "Ooga Boogas." And when she talked to us, which was almost never, she sounded like a normal person, not fake actressy. So we knew she didn't like us anymore.

Maeve also rehearsed the third grade in their dance, which came from Argentina, and its name is the tango. The last day of school, my grade sat in the auditorium watching them. Next, it was our turn. Every one of the third-grade classes was onstage, dancing the tango. First, each class did it separately, then they did it together to "Jealousy," which is the official tango song. When they began to mix it up, all the separate classes dancing, they totally were into it. It was like watching a Broadway musical, they could have been rehearsing a year! They turned together and threw their partners in and out together, and moved their hips like I didn't think little kids knew how.

The audience went crazy. I mean, they must have clapped for five minutes, and in the end, after the third-grade class took their bows in this really cute way, like it was another dance, Maeve ran out from backstage and took a very low show-offy bow. She threw kisses to the audience with a smile on her face as if she won an Oscar. And then when the applause stopped, she threw her hand straight out like a traffic cop and pointed to my class standing on the steps going up to the right side of the stage. The audience thought she was still smiling when she introduced us. But if you were standing where we were and could see her eyes, you could tell that only her lips were smiling. The rest of her face wished we were dead.

Our music, "Lullaby of Broadway," started, and it was like that glare of Maeve's was a curse. As bad as we were before, this was us at our worst. We could have been dancing in glue. Two kids slipped and fell down. Joseph and I were doing okay in comparison. We were practically in step at least. I wanted to prove that I could do *one* thing right. But I could see Joseph was upset. He couldn't take his eyes off Maeve, who was walking off-stage, way away to the back of the auditorium. As if she wanted everyone to know she didn't have anything to do with us.

I could see that out in the audience a lot of them were getting bored. They began talking to each other as if it was a party. Even my mother. She was having one of her conversations with Natasha's mother sitting next to her. My father was taking a nap. So what if we weren't as good as the third grade, these were our parents, they were supposed to pay attention.

It was so unfair! We had worked so hard. On top of the unfairness of me losing Butch to Jenna, it made me mad enough to do something to show how unfair it was. So I imitated Joseph in rehearsal, I went, "Ooga Booga." And waved my hands and started jumping up and down. And Joseph, who was looking miserable a second before, suddenly got this big, all-over-his-face smile, and he went, "Ooga Booga." He started jumping and waving.

And then the other kids, almost every one, started jumping and waving and going, "Ooga Booga." Until the whole class had stopped dancing to "Lullaby of Broadway" and was yelling, "Ooga Booga!"

The audience wasn't talking to each other anymore. They began to clap. The more we "Ooga Booga-ed" to "Lullaby of Broadway," the more they clapped. Soon

they were cheering along with the clapping, so how could we stop "Ooga Booga-ing"? We couldn't. And then Maeve was onstage, jumping up and down with us, but making it into a kind of dance. She was clapping, going "Ooga Booga." She was leading the entire audience in "Ooga Boogas." All her waving and jumping and clapping was as if Maeve wanted them to think that this whole thing was rehearsed and it was her idea in the first place. I should have tripped her, but I didn't.

CHAPTER 19

Spring vacation is supposed to be fun, but not this one. I wasn't having a single minute of fun. Some kids came over for play dates, but even if we ran around a lot, and laughed and looked like we were having fun, it was more pretend fun than actual fun.

I didn't want to call up Jenna, but my mother said I shouldn't hold it against her that she had Butch and I didn't. She told me to be a good sport, even though I had been the best sport in the world in school when she got Butch. I didn't see why I had to go on being a good sport on vacation.

And when I did call up Jenna to forgive her, and for her to invite me over to play with Butch, she couldn't stop showing off how much Butch loved her and how when she called his name, his ears and his nose twitched, and she never saw that happen in class when someone called him. And I said, yes, I saw him do that plenty of times in class. And she said she never saw it, and maybe I was imagining it. And then she didn't even invite me over to play with him. That's not being a good sport. But she didn't have to be, because she didn't have my mother.

Maybe to make me feel better, which wasn't going to happen—why should it?—my mother decided we should go visit my married half-sister, Kate, who lives in Massachusetts. Halley couldn't go because her school has a different vacation from mine. So I was going, but she was going to stay in the city. My mother let her stay two nights at her friend Morgan's. I hated that because I wanted Halley to play with in the car. But then I decided it was better because with only my mother and father, I could have the backseat all to myself and mope.

If my father would only this time give me a break and not make me look out the window. I really didn't get what it was with my father and scenery. I like scenery too, but I think it's better when you're in it than when you're watching it.

Kate and her husband, Chris, live way, way, way up in Massachusetts, so it takes almost a whole day to get there in a car, and no matter how many times we go, we get lost because my mother, who won't let my father drive, has a bad sense of direction and my father's joke is "Your mother has a bad sense of direction and I have no sense of direction."

But it's not so funny when you know that every time you get in a car, you're going to get lost. And they're going to get in a fight over whose fault it is. And if my mother was right about it being my father's fault, he would get very quiet and take a nap. And if my father was right about it being her fault, my mother would remind him of the last time when he was wrong.

So in between getting lost and pretending to look out the window, the real fun in car rides is when they're over. You'd think because my father talks about scenery so much and "Look at this, Julie" and "Look over there, Julie" that he was a teacher of nature who lived outdoors all year hunting and fishing. But he doesn't know the name of one single tree, and he won't go camping because you have to sleep outdoors. The truth is he doesn't like to leave his studio, which is next to my bedroom, where he

drew the pictures for this book. My mother makes him go on car rides, even when he doesn't want to. So why should I have to look out the window just because he says so?

The one good thing about the trip, which made me almost happy but I wasn't ready yet, was that Timmy was coming with us. He had never been in a car before. He had never been out of the house since we got him. Except when he was a kitten and sick, and every other day, almost, my father had to take him to the vet.

He was too small for a kennel when he was a kitten. My father used to put him inside one of his wool socks and carried him in his pocket to the vet. That's as much traveling as Timmy ever did in his life. And now he was going on this car ride to Massachusetts, which took us so long every time we went that my father made a joke out of me asking "Are we there yet?" As if I asked it every five minutes, which was unfair. Because by the time I asked—and I always waited almost until I couldn't stand it—we should have been there. And I don't think I even asked more than two or three times, and then only when I was sure we were lost.

But that was just the normal in the car look-out-the-window-are-we-there-yet-I-think-we're-lost stuff. That's not what made this trip so awful that my father and mother, who joke about everything awful after it's over, didn't joke about this.

CHAPTER 20

Although we didn't know it yet, the awful part began when we were all packed and our stuff was by the door, Timmy's stuff too, like cat food and litter and his litter box, and my father said, "Okay, let's get Timmy and put him in the kennel." And my mother said, "Shouldn't we have done that already?"

And my father said, "If you're impatient, take the bags down to the car and load up."

And my mother said, "Oh no, we're a family and we'll leave together like a family."

Now, I thought I knew exactly where to find Timmy because he followed me around when I was feeding Hammy and Oscar and Turtelini their food for the two days we'd be away, and when I was filling Hammy's water bottle and pouring extra water into Oscar and Turtelini's tanks. Every minute, Timmy was so close, rubbing himself against my leg, that I was scared of tripping over him. "Be careful or I'll trip, Timmy." I didn't say it in a mean way, I said it the way

I always talked to him, as if I'm his best friend or his mother.

"Do we have Timmy?" my mother yelled from the front door. She didn't like to wait. "Julie, go get Timmy," my father said.

But Timmy wasn't by my side anymore. I looked around. I didn't see him. He wasn't anywhere. I searched my bedroom. "Did you find him yet?" my father asked. And when I said no, he told me where to go and how I should look. It was like we were the police. Under the bed, in my bed under the blanket, in the closet, inside my playhouse . . . "Timmy," I said very loud, but it wasn't a yell because I didn't want to scare him.

"Timmy!" my father yelled, and every time he yelled it—ten times or more—it sounded worse. If I was Timmy, I wouldn't have come out.

My mother showed up from the front door. "What's going on here?" and when we told her, she started calling, "Timmy! Nice Timmy, good Timmy." But the way she said it, if I was Timmy, I wouldn't have believed her.

"We'll have to leave him here," my mother said.

"We can't!" I said.

"We may have no choice," my mother said.

"He's never been alone." I started to cry. And that changed my mother's mind because I think she had enough of me crying over the rabbit.

How could a cat who I just saw a couple of minutes ago disappear like that? Me and my father and mother looked in every room, in every closet, under every bed, behind the furniture, under the furniture, under the sink, in the broom closet. "Timmy," we yelled, without trying to be nice anymore.

I never saw Timmy vanish before. But he was never going on a trip before. Maybe he thought he was going to the vet. "We're not going to the vet, Timmy!" I yelled, but I was too excited to sound nice. Wherever he was, I was sure I scared him.

And I was scared too. First, I lose my secret place with my letter in it, and then I lose Timmy. Why couldn't I hold on to things? What else was I going to lose?

"We can't wait any longer," my mother said. She gave me one of her looks that said, "This would be a bad time for you to cry. I really need you not to cry."

If I couldn't cry and we were going to leave without Timmy in a minute, I had to find him *now*. I couldn't lose my secret place *and* my cat. I squinted my eyes closed and tried to see in my brain where he'd hide. My brain said, Go back and look in the kitchen. But there weren't so many places to hide in the kitchen. I had looked under the stove and under the sink and in the broom closet and in the pantry. I followed my brain back into the kitchen, I didn't know what else to do.

He wasn't in any of the places he hadn't been before. I was desperate. I turned around and around and around in the kitchen, which was how I saw what I had seen a hundred times before but didn't think about it: an empty shopping bag my mother brought home from the supermarket that morning. Just standing on the floor next to the kitchen table. Who'd notice an empty shopping bag? My brain noticed.

"Timmy," I said, almost in a whisper.

"Meow" came out of the shopping bag.

CHAPTER 21

I was so used to Timmy the way he was around the house that I forgot he wasn't normal and he wouldn't travel normal. Like, at home, when I called him, he'd hide, and when I didn't have time because of homework, he'd jump in my lap and make me scratch him fifteen minutes. Or that he was hungry all the time except when I opened a can of cat food and he treated it like poison. The tiniest speck of food in his water dish, he wouldn't drink it, so I had to change his water dish five times a day to stop him from rattling it or turning it over on the floor.

Maybe I let myself get too excited that he was going with us to make up for how sad I felt because of Butch. At least I had my own cat, who I didn't need a letter from my parents for him to be with me. So how could I know, no one in the whole wide world could know, you'd have to be the world's biggest genius to figure out how Timmy would make this the worst car ride of my life. My parents' life too.

The big search for him was only the beginning.

Next, he wouldn't let me or my father put him in his cat kennel. He twisted and tried to jump out of my father's hands. My father tried shoving him in feet first. He clawed him, I screamed. My father turned Timmy upside down and squeezed his head in first, and that way jammed him into the kennel. It looked so cruel. Timmy was yelling and trying to bite and scratch. My father was bleeding on both wrists and breathing so loud I thought he was going to faint. Or maybe murder Timmy, if Timmy didn't murder him first.

Timmy wouldn't shut up in the kennel. He went meow, meow, meow all the way down in the elevator. He meowed when my father put him in the backseat with me. When my mother started up the car and we were actually driving on the street, Timmy went crazy with meows. "Can't you do something about that cat?" my mother asked. It wasn't really a question. She knew and I knew and my father knew that as long as the trip took, Timmy would meow. He'd meow all the way up to Massachusetts to my sister Kate's house. That was how many hours of meows I don't even know, but I knew that I should try to shut Timmy up or my mother might drive us off a bridge.

I rocked his cage gently and I said, "Timmy, we're going to have so much fun." And Timmy looked at me as if he always knew that I was waiting to kill him. And he went meow. And he threw up.

And a second after he threw up, he pooped.

"What's that smell?" my mother said.

My father turned around in the front seat to see. "Oh my god," he said. My mother didn't say anything. She just kept driving, but I could see that her hands were on the wheel so tight it was like she was trying to break it off.

"There's a supermarket on the corner of Ninety-third and Amsterdam," my father said. My mother was being very quiet. My father too, he didn't say another word. Their being so quiet made me afraid to talk. What I wanted to ask was why they were going shopping with poop and throw up in the car right next to me. The smell wasn't like anything you ever want to smell in a car. It wasn't like cat poop, it was like a thousand cat poops.

My father got out of the car and went into the supermarket. My mother and I were alone in the car. With Timmy. I looked at my mother's face in the mirror over the steering wheel. She was white and she was biting her lip and her eyes were closed. I had to say something to make her feel better. I thought of "The smell is worse back here," but I decided that wouldn't work. So what I said was "At least he's not meowing anymore." And I smiled. I hoped my mother would see me in her rearview mirror and appreciate that I made a joke to cheer her up.

I saw her looking at me in the mirror. She made a kind of a smile, but I can't be sure, I had never seen that look on her face before. "We made a mistake bringing Timmy," she said to me in the mirror.

"You don't like him," I said, watching to see if her face changed. I hoped it would. But it didn't.

"I like him," she said. It was funny having her sit in front of me, a couple of inches away, and we're not looking at each other. We're looking in the car mirror.

"You don't pet him," I said.

"I don't pet him," she said it back to me.

We were sitting in the car with that smell. But why? We were parked. We could have got out. It was stupid, except I didn't want to leave Timmy. But why did my mother stay?

"Julie, you love animals. I don't. They scare me."

I didn't believe her. "You watch *National Geographic* with me, which is all about animals."

She smiled into the mirror like her real self. "I love

watching *National Geographic* with you. If it's TV, I'm not afraid of animals. I like them because you like them. But I wouldn't watch without you."

It hurt my feelings that she wouldn't watch without me. "You don't like *National Geographic*? It's really good."

"Julie, I wish I could love animals as much as you do. But I love you loving them."

"I love Timmy," I said.

She didn't say anything.

"Are you going to make me give him away?"

"Never!" she almost shouted.

I was having a little trouble with my breathing. "You have to try to love him too," I said.

All of a sudden my mother got out of the car. I didn't understand why. It could have been she saw my father coming back with a shopping bag full of stuff and it reminded her—what was she doing stuck in a smelly car? I said in the nicest voice I had, "I'll be right here, Timmy," and I got out too. I was breathing cat poop in a car for so long I couldn't believe the fresh air. It made my head funny and my legs shaky.

"How'd you do?" my mother asked my father. Outside in the open air, I started to feel bad for my mother, how she looked and everything. I felt bad for Timmy too, I didn't want him to think I was forgetting him just because of how bad I felt for my mother.

My father took Timmy's cage out of the backseat. He put it down on the sidewalk and sat down on the curb next to it. He opened the wire door to the cage. Timmy was scrunched all the way in the back as if he liked lying in poop and throw up and didn't want it to change. My father took a roll of paper towels out of the shopping bag. He unrolled something like six sheets and tore them off the roll. Then he reached into the cage for Timmy. Timmy didn't want to come out. My father reached so far back in the cage he was practically touching the other end. He picked Timmy up by the scruff of his neck—that's the loose fur at the top of his neck, it's not supposed to hurt when you grab a cat there, but I don't believe it.

I said to my father, "Don't!" He dragged Timmy out of the kennel. His fur around his whiskers and down his front was stained. And his chest hairs were wet and tangled, and so was the hair on his front paws and under his belly, which my father wiped with paper towels and then more towels. Timmy's belly hair was short and dripping yuck. He didn't look scared, he looked sad, like he wished he was home. I said, "I'm sorry, Timmy." But I don't think he cared what I said.

My father said, "Julie, I have a job for you." Then he made me take a box of green plastic garbage bags out of the shopping bag and open one of them up. It wasn't as easy as it sounds, and it's something he should have done, but he had his hands full of Timmy, so I didn't say anything.

These green plastic bags are almost impossible to get open. You have to look for the end that opens, which is hard because there's no way of knowing. So the way you find out is, you just keep rubbing the plastic bag back and forth in your hands until you see a little hole open on one end or the other. And that shows you where the top is, and then you slip your finger in and it's easy from then on.

By the time I got it all figured out, my father was glaring at me and saying things like "We don't have all day, Julie," which I don't think was very nice of him. Once I had the bag open, and I opened it really wide to show my father I was trying my best, he threw in the yucky pieces of paper towel that came from wiping off Timmy. The towels were disgusting and I was scared that a piece of one might touch my hand by accident when my father threw it in. But it never did, or I would have dropped the bag and run away screaming.

My mother smoked a cigarette and watched my father and me from almost two cars away. She didn't say anything during the whole cleanup except once, near the very end, when she said it like it was a warning: "This day is going to improve."

After Timmy was as clean as he was going to get, my father handed him over to me. I think Timmy was ashamed of the trouble he caused, so he stayed still in my arms and didn't move an inch. My father took out a spray cleaner, one of the things he bought at the supermarket, and sprayed it into Timmy's kennel, all over, even the roof. Then he wiped everything down with paper towels, picked up the poop and the throw up with paper towels, and sprayed the whole thing again and wiped it off again.

He scrunched the yucky paper towels into a ball and shoved them in the plastic bag, which I couldn't open for him anymore because I was holding on to Timmy.

By this time he had used up half a roll of towels and the green bag smelled like the inside of our car. My father twisted the bag closed and tried to make a knot in it, but every time he tried, the knot slipped and came loose. Which is funny, because people think he's an artist so he should be good with his hands, but he's no good at knots or mostly anything else that other fathers can do with their hands. The only thing my father knows how to do with his hands is draw cartoons.

My mother said, "I'll do that." So my father gave her the plastic bag and took back Timmy. She's the one in our family who's good at knots. My father squeezed Timmy back into his kennel. Except for one quiet meow, he didn't even complain. He just lay down and closed his eyes.

"Can we leave?" my mother said after dumping the plastic bag in a big wire basket on the corner.

I got back in the car next to Timmy, wishing that I had three wishes. My first wish would have been that this trip could be over before it began.

CHAPTER 22

We were on the road for it couldn't be an hour when the smell came back. I noticed first because I was closest to Timmy. I promised myself I would die of the smell before I told my parents. I looked in the front seat to see if they noticed. I saw my father almost turn his head to look back, but he stopped. His body got sort of stiff. He went back to looking out the window and didn't say anything. A minute later, the smell was worse than the time that made us stop before. My mother was so quiet I could almost hear it. Nobody made a sound. It was like we all made up our minds we weren't going to mention it—the whole rest of the trip we were going to live inside a toilet.

A couple of miles later I couldn't stand it. I said, "Mommy."

"I know," she said, and drove the car off the road.

"Here we go again," my father said. He made it sound like a joke, but nobody thought it was funny. We were someplace out in the country—I don't know where—on this highway with another highway on the other side going in a back-to-the-city direction. In between both highways was a lawn, kind of. This long parky thing but without flowers or trees. Actually, nothing was on it. It was just there to split up the highway, so cars could get off like we did when they ran out of gas, or something else was wrong. But we were the first, I bet, who got off for cat poop.

My mother was in a better mood this time. It was like she had gotten used to the trip being the worst trip we ever took, but what could we do? We couldn't kill Timmy. So why not let my father clean up the poop because that's what he was an expert in. And let her tie up the garbage bag because that's what she was an expert in. And we could do this for fifty more poops until we got to Kate's house in Massachusetts, where I knew the first thing when we got there is they would ask for a glass of wine.

But my father was in a rotten mood. It was like he didn't mind cleaning up the poop that once because he was good at it. But he didn't like doing it again, and then again, and he had to keep doing it and doing it because it was his job. He was nearly finished with the cleanup, which he was getting faster at, when a police car drove off the highway and parked right behind our car, and a policeman in a brown uniform and riding boots got out. He was very big. He walked toward us

kind of slow, but like he was interested.
My father, even though he's six feet,
looked small next to him.

"Do you need help?" the policeman asked my father, who was sitting
on the grass with his arm very far into
the cat kennel. I had hold of Timmy.

My father looked embarrassed,
like he'd been caught doing something
he was ashamed of. He didn't answer
the policeman. He didn't say anything, or even look at him. I'm only a
kid, but I know you have to answer a
policeman if he asks you a question.
And this policeman was trying to
be nice in spite of being big enough
to be scary.

My father is not very good with people he doesn't
know. If he was alone, or just with me, he could have
gotten us arrested. But my mother is great with everybody the first time. She came over to the policeman,
and soon she was in the middle of telling him about
Timmy as if it was a joke and not how she really felt.
The two of them made jokes about Timmy and laughed
like they were getting to be friends. And I could see my
father looking more embarrassed. Or maybe mad. And
the policeman was laughing and telling my mother a

story about *his* dog in *his* car. I wanted to ask what kind of dog because I was getting a Chihuahua, and wouldn't it have been a coincidence if this policeman had a Chihuahua too? But my mother was laughing too much for me to interrupt, as if this was the funniest story she ever heard. And she gave the policeman a cigarette. My father had just finished cleaning up the kennel, so he took Timmy out of my arms, I guess to put him back in, but he let him go.

I don't mean it was on purpose, though that's almost what it looked like. I mean, he took him from me with the wrong grip, and Timmy, who was very quiet up to that second, just all of a sudden was on the ground running away. Right toward the highway with all this traffic.

My mother screamed. I don't know what I did. I think I started running. We were all running. No, not my mother, but the rest of us. Me and my father and this big, fat, stupid policeman who started the whole thing.

Back and forth, we chased Timmy up and down this dopey lawn we were on. He ran as if he was heading right onto the highway, and then he turned, and this time he ran toward the opposite side of the highway, going in the other direction. He didn't care where he was going. He would go anywhere except toward us.

We called to him and chased him: "Timmy! Timmy!" But not my mother. She stood still, watching. Why wasn't she running? I was stumbling a lot because I was crying so hard I couldn't see where I was going. His third or fourth time around, Timmy ran right into me, bumping into my leg. He was gone before I got the idea that this thing that bumped me was my cat. My father called him and cursed him at the same time, using words I'm not even supposed to know. I was mad at him because he was calling these words to my cat who *he* let go of.

It must have been over five minutes and we weren't getting any closer to catching him. All of a sudden my mother said real loud, but it wasn't like a shout or a yell, "Everybody stop. Stop running." And everybody stopped. The policeman too. And he didn't have to. He's not in our family.

"Please don't anybody move," my mother said, this time in a quieter voice.

And we didn't move. As soon as we stopped running, we all got what her idea was. We stood stiff on this long green lawn like we were paralyzed. The policeman too. With traffic zooming by on both sides of us and Timmy running almost into it and then not. After two minutes of standing still like that, Timmy slowed down to a walk, then came over to my mother. He started rubbing himself against her leg. Between her teeth that were clenched, she said, "Will somebody get this cat?"

The policeman got to Timmy before me and picked him up fast, before he could get away again. My father opened the kennel and the policeman put Timmy in. My father looked even more embarrassed than before. He still hadn't said a word to the policeman. My mother came over and made jokes to the policeman about our big chase, as if there was something funny about it, which there wasn't. The policeman took off in his police car, smoking a cigarette she gave him.

CHAPTER 23

The last part of the trip to Kate's, Timmy was the best cat in the world. He didn't poop or throw up or meow once. He was so quiet I looked through the bars of his cage to make sure he was alive.

I was very sad for him. So I made up this story to cheer him up. I wrote it in my head to tell him later, though. Because I get embarrassed if my parents hear me talk to my pets. It doesn't matter to my father, but my mother calls up all her friends and tells them what I said.

"Once upon a time there was a cat named Timmy who was so nervous all the time and scared too if you said 'Boo!' to him he'd faint. But it wasn't his fault. Timmy was an orphan and the way that happened is once in the middle of the night, a robber came and kidnapped him from his mommy and daddy. But the robber didn't like Timmy, so he let him go. And Timmy didn't have any place to go, so he ran back and forth a lot on the street and he almost got run over a hundred times, but he was lucky. And then one day Timmy goes to a house in the woods in the country and a dog lived there. A Chihuahua named Jessie. And Jessie loved Timmy and Timmy loved Jessie. And they played together all the time, so many games you can't even count. So everybody was surprised because dogs and cats aren't supposed to be best friends, but this was a Great Experiment. And it worked. So Timmy wasn't a scaredy-cat anymore. And he wasn't an orphan anymore because Jessie was his family now. So Timmy was happy from then on forever and ever and ever and ever. The end."

CHAPTER 24

My father called Kate on the cell phone to say we'd be late. But we're always late. It's for different reasons every time, but most of the time we're late.

We got to Massachusetts when it was almost dark. Kate's house is small and in the woods, but not very woodsy woods, so it's not creepy or anything. It's just enough woods to make you know you're in the country and not in a small town with lots of little houses and stores, one next to the other that makes it look crowded like a city but not as cool.

If I didn't live in an apartment on the twelfth floor where you look out the window when it gets hot and you can see the rooftops of all the buildings on your block and the next block and the one after that, and you see people almost without anything on sunbathing or having parties out there or on terraces, and they play music that's too far away to know what it is but they dance sometimes to it, so if I couldn't see that or the river or actually the part of it I can see outside my father's studio window, and the sun sets there and you can see it through the two buildings that are in the way of the river but not all the way in the way, but you can see enough to see the water and boats go by and the sunset, if I couldn't see all that, then I think I'd want to live like Kate and Chris and my niece, Maddy, in a house in the woods because it reminds me of a fairy tale.

I'm Maddy's aunt, which is funny, because I'm only four years older than she is. Kate is closer to my mother's age than she is to mine. We're sisters, but Kate has a different mother, Judy, who my father, before he got married to my mother, was married to. Way before Halley was born. And she's seven years older than me, so Kate's way older than that, but she doesn't look it. I think she looks young enough to be my sister, even if she is a mother. She has red hair, which she wears long. Halley's a blonde. Maddy's a redhead. My mother's hair is brown. My father doesn't have any hair. He's bald. My hair is black and curly because I'm adopted and brown.

We got to Kate's house and Maddy was the first one out like always. She calls me JuJu. Every time I go she has something new in the house to show me because Chris knows how to make stuff. She had a little guest house he made for her and a tree house. It made me jealous. I would be even more jealous, but Chris makes stuff for me too. Anything I asked him for, when he had time, he made. My mother said, "Don't take advantage of Chris." But if he didn't make stuff for me, who would? My father couldn't make anything except pictures, and I guess that's good for a job or to show off to my friends, but it wasn't what I needed.

Chris made Maddy things she needed. And if my father couldn't, and my mother tried but was no good at it either, and Chris wanted to . . . It's not as if I forced him, I'm only a kid. So why make myself sad and say no? If I said yes, only my mother got mad, and she'd forget in five minutes and tell funny stories. And my father was embarrassed he couldn't make anything, so he was glad I had Chris.

Maddy was all excited because Kate had plans for tomorrow. We were going to a farm. It was about an hour away in mountains they call the Berkshires, with goats and cows and chickens and pigs and ducks. Me and Maddy could ride ponies and I could feed the animals—Maddy too, but she mainly wanted to do it because of me. The idea of feeding animals got me so excited I couldn't sleep. I stayed up late thinking about how I'd feed the goats. I never fed a goat. I'm not sure what you do exactly. That's okay, the farmer would show me. And even if he didn't, when I'm there on the farm—me and the goats—I'll just know.

CHAPTER 25

We couldn't take Timmy with us. We left him at Kate's house, locked up downstairs in the cellar with food and water and kitty litter. Chris said we'd only be gone three or four hours, so he'd be fine. He had a million places to hide down there, so he should be happy, like between the washer and dryer, or behind the furnace, or under the water tank. There was even a basket of dirty laundry he could crawl right to the bottom of. For the first time on this trip, I didn't have to worry about him.

CHAPTER 26

It was called The Farm on the Falls because there was a waterfall right in the middle of the farm, and you had to cross a bridge—no, two bridges, a big one and a little one. There was a creek that was narrow in the beginning and then it got so wide it would take you a couple of minutes to swim across even if you were a very fast swimmer. But the water was so cold you wouldn't want to go swimming. It was more just to look at, because it was dark blue and moving really fast over a million little rocks and branches with leaves but no flowers. I mean, there wasn't a smooth inch in that stream, so even if you were the best swimmer, you'd still cut yourself up on all those rocks and branches that stuck out and scratched you. I bet the best swimmer would bleed to death before he got to the other side of the creek.

It wasn't a fancy farm. Mainly, the opposite. I thought it was great-looking, but if you didn't love animals, I'd have to agree with my father that it was disgusting. He didn't say that. He wouldn't because he knew it would have hurt my feelings. But he's fussier about these things than my mother and me. Or Kate and Chris, who live in the country, so they're kind of used to mud everywhere, and dirty-looking barns that I don't think are that dirty. It has to be a little messy if you live with animals.

My father lived in apartments in New York his whole life, so he doesn't like it the same way I do, even though I also live in an apartment, but with a zoo in my room. So I'm used to things messy. Anyhow, after five minutes it was magic to me. I mean, after all the bad stuff—Butch the rabbit, and Timmy pooping and running away—this made up for it. Every smelly barn or stable was like somebody gave me a Christmas present I couldn't get open fast enough.

I couldn't stand still. I wanted to go everywhere right away. I took Maddy into a shed and we saw two baby lambs just born that day—that morning! Ten o'clock that morning, an hour and a half before we got there! Feeding off their mommy, they were small, but I thought pretty big for something that just got born. And standing up! They could walk! I couldn't at that age, are you kidding? Maddy couldn't either. I wanted to take them home, they were so cuddly. I wanted to take the whole farm home.

One of the boy farmers showed us a blue bin where they had bags full of crusty bread. Maddy and I shared a bag and fed it to the goats. They were behind a wire

fence, and as soon as they saw
us coming, they stopped what
they were doing and came
running to the fence and stuck
their noses out between the wires.

Maddy was scared of them until
she saw me feed one. I took a piece of
bread out and I held it in my hand and
the goat stuck his whole mouth right in my
hand and went snort, snort and the bread was gone. But
he wanted more. No matter how much bread you gave
those goats, they were hungry for more. I don't know
what made them so hungry, they just sat around all day.

I guess if you're a free goat, you just go out and eat
what you feel like whenever you feel like it. But if you're
a goat stuck inside a fence, you can't eat anytime you
want, so you gobble up anything you can because you
don't know when they'll let you eat next.

Maddy watched how I fed the goat and then she said,
"Look, JuJu." And she fed the next goat. So we took
turns, because she didn't like to miss me feeding my goat
and I liked to look at her feeding her goat. One time we
decided to have an eating contest where we counted to
three and both of us fed our goats at the same time. And
the goat who finished first was the winner. But they finished at the same time, it didn't work. We played the game
three times and they always finished at the same time.

Maddy wanted to feed the baby lambs, but I said they'd only feed off their mother because they were just born. But she wanted to try, so we went back to the lamb house and she called and called the lambs to come and eat out of her hand. Her hand is so small that she could shove it through the wire fence. My hand was too big for the lamb fence. But it didn't matter, the baby lambs were asleep and even though Maddy shouted—I told her not to—they weren't going to wake up for Maddy or anybody.

So I said, "Let's feed the pigs." But a girl farmer said, "We're not allowed to feed the pigs." Maddy wanted to anyway, but I told her she couldn't, and she listened to me because I'm her aunt. The pigs were almost as big as horses. They were scary, they were so big. Cows and horses can be a lot bigger and they won't be scary because that's how they come, they're supposed to be big, that's how you think of cows and horses. But even though pigs come in different sizes, when you see an enormous pig it doesn't look right. It's more like a horror-movie pig that maybe got gigantic by being injected in a laboratory.

One of the pigs was black and the other was pink, and they just stood there in their pig hole not moving. They were amazingly clean, cleaner maybe than anything else that I saw on the farm. The girl farmer said they were friendly, but Maddy and I didn't wait to find out. I liked it better looking at them from far away. It was a little too scary up close.

Next they took us on a trail ride, and that was scarier than the pigs or anything else that happened. My mother went, and Kate and Chris and Maddy. One girl farmer rode in front of us on a horse and another girl farmer rode behind us on a horse. My father didn't go because he won't ride horses. He has a bad back. It goes out and he can't get out of bed for a week. But even if he had a good back, he wouldn't ride on a horse.

Maddy and me, they gave ponies. Mine was Wendy, hers was Smokey. They made us put on helmets. The trail we were on went straight up, it felt like a mountain with mud and rocks everywhere. The horses with their hooves kicked rocks that rolled down the hill. And if you were riding behind the other horses, the rocks rolled right into your horse. So my poor little Wendy was dodging rocks like it was an avalanche. If she tripped, she would have gone rolling down the hill like one of the rocks, and me with her. And I only had on a helmet to protect my head. I didn't dare think of the poor rest of my body.

My mother started out on the trail ride talking a lot—her and Kate—and making jokes. But then she got quieter and then very quiet as the trail got windier. She had to duck to keep from hitting her head on tree branches that stuck out low all over the trail. If you missed ducking, it could knock you off your horse. And you'd roll down into the woods that were more rocks than woods. So my mother didn't talk anymore until the ride was over.

It was a miracle nobody got hurt on that ride. When we got back, my father was sitting on a tree stump, smiling, I think, because he didn't have to go.

I saw Kate whisper something to Maddy. Then she said, "Julie, Maddy has something to show you." Maddy held out her hand. "Come, JuJu." Sometimes Maddy likes to tell me what to do and I let her because I'm a good aunt.

Maddy took me to a shed next to a long box full of water that horses drink out of. I didn't remember seeing this shed before. It was so tiny my head was almost up to the ceiling, and there was hay all over the floor. Maddy took me to the back, where it was dark except for one part that was lit up from a little window just under the roof, like a square hole that the sun came through.

"Look, JuJu," Maddy said. A big, fat, gray-and-white cat was lying in the middle of the sun spot, and under her belly sucking away like crazy were two of the most adorable kittens you ever saw. And lying all over each other, I counted three other kittens asleep. I wanted to take them all home.

Kate had come up behind us and leaned over me to get a better look. "The mother's name is Mitzi. Can you guess how old the litter is?"

"A week?" I said.

"That's really good, Julie. It's ten days."

I asked Kate if I could go closer. She said, "Yes."

Maddy said, "Me too," but I had to hold her back, she tried to go too close. We stood and watched a long time, I don't know how long. The kittens weren't doing much, but I didn't care, all I wanted was to watch and watch and watch some more. Kate said, "I think it's time to go, Julie."

Just then, one of the kittens started rolling over and

over in the hay. She was one of the tiniest. She had a gray head and body but was all white around her mouth and nose and part of her neck, with a big white spot on her chest. Everywhere else she was dark gray, except she had white, white paws.

She rolled right at us—I didn't think it was on purpose—but when she was only this much away from me and Maddy, she stood up and looked at me. She shook the hay off and lifted her head, this tiny little head, and her big eyes looked straight at me.

"She's looking at JuJu," Maddy said.

"Julie, I think it's all right to pick her up," Kate said. She sounded as if she could be wrong and get us yelled at. But I didn't wait for her to take it back. I fell down on my knees in the hay. Maddy too. "Kitty, kitty, kitty, kitty," I said. And she came to me, the way Timmy never does.

She rubbed her head against the side of my arm. I looked at Kate. "Can I really pick her up?" Maddy was looking scared. I was scared too, but I held the kitty in my arms for a second or two, then I wasn't anymore. She didn't squirm or meow or anything. Timmy would have twisted and turned, and if I let him go he'd be a mile away in a second.

This kitten was the bravest I ever saw. Not that I've seen so many, but I've seen a lot. And she was the bravest. She didn't even know me, but she let me hold her. Even kiss her. I brought her right up to my face and rubbed my nose against her nose. She looked right at me like it was okay. Then I let Maddy do it. I could see she was nervous about it, but I held the kitten right up to her face. She rubbed her nose against the kitten's nose.

"Okay," Kate said. I put the kitty down, though I hated to. She shook herself and walked back to her mother and all her brothers and sisters sitting in a circle, which she sat down in the middle of. She looked at me waving goodbye. I waved and waved and waved. I would have waved until my arm fell off. Or at least until she looked away, which she wasn't doing.

"Okay," Kate said. That meant we had to leave.

Going back to Kate's house in her car, Chris was driving and he said, "Julie, wouldn't you love to have a kitten?"

And I didn't have to think about it. I said, "No."

My father laughed. "Oh, sure," he said.

But I meant it. I wanted a kitten, but if I was going to have a dog, then I couldn't. I could take care of one cat and one dog, but I didn't know how I could take care of two cats and a dog. Besides, I was saving my asks. I was afraid if I used one up on the kitten, what would happen to my dog?

CHAPTER 27

All night long I woke up and changed my mind about the kitty and fell asleep and woke up again and changed it back and fell asleep and woke up again and changed it again. When my mother told me in the morning it was time to get up and get dressed and get packed to go back to New York, I said, "I don't want to go."

But I did want to go, kind of. I was tired of not being able to make up my mind. In New York I wouldn't worry about making up my mind. But I wasn't really ready, because I wanted to go one more time to the farm. I wanted to see my kitten.

I woke up that morning with a secret plan. I was going to work at the farm when I got older, maybe in the summer when I was a teenager. I would be a girl farmer like the two girl farmers there, who'd be old when I was a teenager so they'd need me to take their place. And my kitten would be grown up. But the first day I worked there, she'd know me. She'd run over.

I made up a whole story in my head about how this

big cat—this gray-and-white spotted cat—ran over to me and jumped into my arms. And everything I did that summer, feed the goats, feed the cows, take little children out on trail rides, my cat came with me. I even made up a name for her. Jessie.

CHAPTER 28

Kate made us breakfast. But I wasn't too hungry so my mother said, "Katie made us this nice breakfast, eat something, Julie."

But I couldn't. And my father said, "You've got to eat something."

But you shouldn't have to eat something just to be polite. I mean, I didn't think it was rude to not eat Kate's breakfast. If you always have to eat something because it's polite, then what's being hungry all about? You may as well not ever be hungry and only eat when it's polite.

Anyhow, after everyone but me ate breakfast, Kate looked embarrassed. She said, "I want to read you something."

"It's her children's book," Chris said.

"It's about me!" Maddy said. We all sat down. The grown-ups sat on chairs, me and Maddy sat on the floor.

Kate said, "Are you sure you want to hear this? It's very rough." Kate had never written a book before.

This was her first. It was about a little red-haired girl who had to be Maddy, who had a mother who sounded just like Kate. And the little girl's favorite color was pink, so she wore pink, and her room was painted pink, and all her furniture was pink, and so was her bed and everything else. So when the mother went into the bedroom looking for the little girl, she couldn't find her. She was invisible in all that pink.

I didn't think it was a very realistic story. I mean, I know how Timmy could get lost in a room, but how could Maddy, especially if she's not playing hide-and-seek? And the girl in the story, I don't think she was trying to hide. But if she was, and it was a game, it could happen. Even though it wasn't realistic, I thought it was good. And my mother and father laughed at practically every sentence. My mother "Oohed" a lot too, so it had to be good.

CHAPTER 29

This is what I did with Maddy that whole last morning after we ate breakfast—we looked for Timmy in the cellar.

It was my father's idea. "Let's get an early start," he said. You can't start too early to look for Timmy, we found that out already. So two hours before we were supposed to leave, my father walked us down to the cellar. "Any other volunteers?" he shouted to my mother and Kate and Chris. They laughed. Even my mother.

We looked between the washer and dryer, and behind. And behind the furnace and under the water heater. My father said, "Maybe we're going to have to leave Timmy with you, Maddy." He was kidding, but I think Maddy was hoping he wasn't. She didn't have any pets, but neither did I when I was five.

It was Maddy who actually found him just when I was starting to worry. He was in the basket of dirty laundry that I went through twice already, but I guess I didn't look hard enough. And when he looked like he was about to escape, Maddy grabbed and hugged him and said, "You want to come live with me, Timmy?"

Well, that's when we stopped being lucky. Because Timmy twisted free, and then we were chasing him all over the cellar like this was a game he liked to play. I got scared for my father, who yelled, "I can't live like this!" And his face got redder than I ever saw it. Even so, he was the one who caught Timmy when he was trying to jump into the dryer.

We left an hour late, but we're always leaving an hour late. It was still too early for lunch, but I was hungry from running around looking for Timmy. Kate would have made us sandwiches, but my mother said, "Don't be silly." So she didn't.

And then Kate felt bad about it, so she made as many as she could as fast as she could when we were packing up the car. So I had half an egg-salad sandwich, except it was on wheat bread and I like white. My father had the other half, which he finished before we got in the car, he was so starving. My mother said she didn't want anything, but the way she looked at my father chewing up his sandwich, I was pretty sure she was lying.

We had lots of chips for the car, and water and soda, and we didn't forget Timmy's stuff either—the paper towels, the spray cleaner, and plenty of plastic bags for when he pooped and threw up.

Timmy was in his kennel next to me, meowing like crazy. I couldn't tell how my mother was feeling. I mean, she sounded real happy, talking a lot, I mean almost more than I wanted to hear about the farm, and did I miss it and "I bet you can't wait to go back for a visit."

My father was also too excited, going on about all the animals on the farm, which wasn't what I needed to hear right now, because I wasn't going to the farm, I was going back to New York. And Timmy would poop in his kennel and the smell would kill us and we'd have to stop the car and clean him up. So what were my parents so happy about?

My mother was almost starting the car down the driveway when a second before, in the middle of all our "Goodbyes" and "Thank yous" and "We had a great times" and "I love yous," Kate said, "Oh, my goodness, I nearly forgot!" She turned around, just like that, and ran back to the house. And Maddy and Chris ran back after her. What was there back in the house?

"I wonder what she forgot," my mother said.

"It can't be that important. Let's go," my father said.

"We don't want to be rude, we may as well wait," my mother said.

Something was weird about the way they were talking, like they didn't mean what they were saying, like it was acting in a play. I didn't get it.

And then I saw Kate, Maddy, and Chris come out on their porch together. They were carrying something—I mean, Maddy was—in a shoebox. I couldn't tell what it was. But my mother started giggling and my father turned around in the front seat and smiled at me. It was such a big smile it almost jumped off his face.

My mother lowered my backseat window by pushing the button near her window. Maddy was almost up to us when she took the top off the shoebox. I saw what was in it. I screamed. It was my cat, Jessie!

Maddy was holding her. She had her in her arms. She was holding Jessie. Where did she come from? Did they bring her from the farm to say goodbye? I didn't know what was happening.

Maddy leaned over. The top of her head just reached the window. She held out Jessie in her hands. Her two arms poked through the window as far as they could go. She dropped Jessie into my lap.

What was happening? Why was this cat in my car in my lap? Did they bring her to say goodbye? How could I say goodbye and go back to New York now? I could have left her behind if I didn't see her, but I couldn't let her go now. It was mean to tease me this way, didn't they know that?

Kate poked her head through the window. She was holding Maddy. I was holding Jessie. I wasn't going to give her up, no matter what Kate said. She said, "They told me at the farm that they had one kitten too many, and did I know any little girl who wanted one?"

"*I WANT ONE!*" I shouted. "*Me! Me! Me!*" Everyone in and out of the car was laughing, but I didn't see anything funny. What was so funny?

My mother leaned over and touched my face the way she does. "Julie, this is your cat. It's a gift from Katie and Chris and Maddy."

Timmy in his kennel went meow. But it was a quiet meow, the nicest meow I ever heard out of him. I think he was saying, "Hello, Jessie."

CHAPTER 30

We got home two hours late, but we always get home late, and this time it wasn't our fault. Timmy pooped three times and we had to stop on the road and clean up. But my mother hardly got upset. It was as if she was getting used to it by now, like Jessie changed her mind about cats.

When we were off the road and me and my father were cleaning up, my mother was holding Jessie on her lap in the front seat of the car. And she was petting her and she even talked to her. I think she talked more to Jessie while we cleaned up than she talked to Timmy in his whole life.

She still didn't know how to pet a cat right. I mean, she did it in the wrong direction, up not down. But it didn't matter to Jessie. She was a kitten, what did *she* care? She purred. "She's purring at me!" my mother yelled at us through the car window. I was outside with my father by the side of the road, holding open a green plastic bag while my father was cleaning up the last of the mess Timmy made.

We walked in the house and I couldn't believe it—Betty was back! I was so happy! I mean, I walked in the door and there she was, it was like everything was normal again. Betty was my babysitter from when I was a month old, like a week or two after I was adopted and brought home.

I hadn't seen Betty in almost a year, though we talked long distance on the phone every three weeks, sometimes more. Last year my mother bought her a house in her hometown in Brazil for her to retire in. So she left us to go back and live with her brother Luiz. The plan was when I got older, I would go visit them.

Betty's real name is Elizabeth. Her friends in her church call her Beth. We call her Betty. I miss her all the time. And she misses me all the time. I know because that's mostly what we talk about on the phone.

Our apartment hadn't been cleaned practically since Betty left. But now it was beautiful. Or getting better anyway. She had been home for a whole day while we were up at Kate's and I don't think she ever stopped vacuuming.

She was retired, she wasn't supposed to vacuum. But when she came all this way to see us, she was ashamed of how the place looked. So even if she didn't work for us anymore, she cleaned the house.

I made Betty stop cleaning because I couldn't wait to show Jessie to her. And Timmy, she didn't know either! Or any of my animals! She had gone home to Brazil a couple of weeks before I started the zoo in my room. So I did all the cleaning up after my pets, which I wouldn't have had to do if Betty still worked for us. It wasn't until I took her in to show her where Hammy and Turtelini and Oscar lived that I saw what a cheat it was that Betty retired just when I needed her the most.

"Can't you come back?" I asked her, practically begged her. I could see she was worried about something, almost from the time we came in the door. Maybe it was that she wanted to unretire and not go back to Brazil. And she felt bad for her brother Luiz. That was okay, he'd get used to it.

"I have to talk to your mama and papa," Betty said. I went back with her into the kitchen. My father had taken Timmy out of his cage to let him get to know Jessie a little, so they could get acquainted and be friends. Except Jessie was sitting right in the middle of the floor all alone.

"Where's Timmy?" I asked.

My mother shook her head. They were sharing a glass of wine, him and her.

"Timmy's disappeared," my father said. I could see Timmy could stay disappeared as far as my father went. No one was going to look for him today anymore. Poor Timmy. He wasn't even interested that he had a new friend we brought home to make him feel better.

CHAPTER 31

"Something come, you don't know," Betty said to my mother. "It come when I clean. You see."

"Can it wait?" my father said. He looked very tired.

"You come," Betty said. Betty was not bossy, so when she sounded bossy, like this wasn't something you could wait to do tomorrow, they knew they had to do it. We followed Betty down the hall to the guest bathroom. The door was closed, but it's never closed. Now it was. Betty opened it. Butch the rabbit was sleeping on the floor of our bathroom. *Butch!* I had Butch! How did he get here? I had everything I ever wanted!

Maybe not my dog, but I had everything else. How come?

The more Betty explained it, the more I didn't understand what she was talking about. She said Jenna's father came to our house with Butch in a cage. Betty hadn't been in our house five minutes when he showed up. He told her he left a bunch of messages on our answering machine, but he couldn't wait, he had to bring Butch for us to take care of the rest of spring break. He said Jenna's grandfather was sick, and maybe dying, and the whole family had to go to Minneapolis right now, that minute. They were waiting downstairs in a cab. They were on their way to the airport. They had to leave. So they brought Butch over for me to take care of.

"Did Jenna's father leave a note for us?" my mother asked.

Betty shook her head no.

"Didn't he leave a number for us to call him?" my father asked. "Or a number in Minneapolis?"

"We don't have to call him," I said. This was everything I ever wanted.

My mother didn't look happy. I hate it when I'm happy and she's not. It means I'm not going to be happy very long.

"There's something wrong with this rabbit." Why did she have to say that? Butch looked all right to me. So what if he was just lying there, not moving. That was okay. That's the way he was a lot in the classroom. His eyes were open, weren't they? So he was fine. Okay, he wasn't staring at much, but maybe that's normal for rabbits when they're not outside. What's there to stare at? The toilet? The sink? The bathtub? Butch was fine.

My mother gave my father one of those looks that I hate. "Let's talk in the kitchen," she told him.

"I think your mother's right, this is a sick rabbit," my father said. I hated it when they agreed with each other against me. I couldn't understand how they could walk away from Butch. But all right, if that's what they wanted.

Betty and I stayed in the bathroom with Butch. Betty had some lettuce she got out of the refrigerator to feed him, but he didn't look at it. I put my face practically on top of him so he could recognize me from school. "Hello, Butch," I said. "Butch, Butch?"

Butch wasn't looking at me or anywhere. His eyes were open, but it didn't look like he saw anything. I wondered what my mother had to talk to my father about in the kitchen. Was Butch going to die? Is that what she wanted to tell him? In a day or two, Butch was going to get better. Timmy didn't die, *he* got better. In our house, we're lucky. Sick animals get better. I knew that, so why didn't my mother?

I asked Betty to keep watching Butch, because it was important to find out what my mother was saying to my father. My father was talking when I got to the kitchen. I stood outside the door and listened.

"I can't believe it," he was in the middle of saying. They were sitting the way they always do, on opposite sides of the kitchen table.

My mother said, "What are we going to do?"

My father said, "I have to think about it."

My mother said, "There's one way to find out."

"What?" my father said.

"Call them," my mother said.

"They're in Minneapolis," my father said.

Now I got it. They were talking about how Jenna's grandfather was dying so she and her parents had to go to Minneapolis. And that's how come I got Butch.

"I don't think they're in Minneapolis," my mother said.

"Yes, they are. That's what they told Betty!" I said.

My mother was surprised to see me standing in the
kitchen door. Her look got serious, I mean scary. "Julie,
I hope I'm wrong, but I think Jenna's mommy and
daddy made up that story when they saw how sick
Butch was and they didn't want to take responsibility."

"We'll feed him with an eyedropper like we did
Timmy."

"Butch is not our responsibility, he's Jenna's," my
mother said.

"But they're in Minneapolis!" I yelled.

"You've got an adorable new little kitten," my mother said.

"I know Butch longer!" I didn't mean to, but I was yelling.

"You see what these people got us into?" my mother said.

"We don't know for sure," my father said.

"He is so my responsibility! I'll show you." I ran back to my room. I was trying not to cry.

I grabbed my book bag. I shook out all the junk in it onto the floor, even a library book I was looking for to take to Kate's house, and I couldn't find it. I closed my eyes. This had to work. I put my hand into the empty book bag. I made a wish. I felt around. In a second, I found the secret pocket. The letter of permission was right where I put it. It was magic! It was proof that Butch belonged with *me*.

I ran with it into the kitchen to prove to my mother that Butch was really my responsibility because he would have been at our house and not Jenna's, except I couldn't find the letter. All I had to do was remind her. She was the one who wrote the letter. The second I was back in the kitchen, I waved the letter at my mother. She had her finger to her lips, shushing me, so she could listen to my father on the phone.

"I told you they're not there," he said.

"Let it ring," my mother said.

"I let it ring ten times. They're in Minneapolis," my father said. And then he said, "Hello, this is Julie's father."

My father pushed the speaker button, so we could hear who it was. "We thought you were in Minneapolis."

Nobody said anything, and then there was this kind of a laugh. It was Jenna's mother. She said, "Yes. Yes. That's right. We were going to call you. We didn't have to go."

My father looked at my mother. She rolled her eyes.

"I'm very glad to hear you didn't have to go. I'll bring the rabbit back."

"No!" I shouted. My mother squeezed my hand to make me shut up.

"Hold on, I'll put my husband on," said Jenna's mother.

We waited a long time and no one got on the other end. Then I heard, "Hi, sorry about the confusion." It was Jenna's father. "My wife and I were thinking, Why don't you save yourself the trouble of bringing him back and keep the rabbit?"

My mother covered my mouth with her hand just as I was shouting, "Yes!"

I saw my father smile at the phone, which is a smile he gets when he thinks he's going to say something funny. "I wish we could take care of the rabbit for you, but my Uncle Louie is dying in Hoboken. And everyone's downstairs in the car waiting to go. I'll drop Butch off on the way. You'd better take him to a vet tomorrow. You don't want him to die on you."

Jenna's father shouted, "Listen, you—"

My father said, "We're on our way" and hung up the phone.

I couldn't believe my father would do that to me. I screamed, "I hate you!"

My mother tried to hug me, but I couldn't stand her touching me. I ran back to Betty in the bathroom and slammed the door. I yelled at her, "Lock it! Lock it!" I forgot the bathrooms in our apartment don't lock.

My mother and father tried to come in, but I stood in the doorway, blocking it. I wouldn't let them in. My mother bent down and held my shoulders. She wanted to look in my eyes, but I wasn't going to let her. I looked down at the floor.

"Julie, Butch is sick. I hope he gets better. But what Jenna's parents did is very cruel. They didn't want to be responsible for Butch dying while they had him, so they made up a lie and brought him to us so they wouldn't be blamed if something happened."

I didn't care why they brought Butch. I deserved him and now I had him and they were giving him back. I didn't understand what they were talking about, it was the meanest thing they ever did. If something happens that you want to happen, does it matter if it's a bad reason it happened? Who cares about the reason, as long as what should happen but didn't does?

Besides, my father didn't have a sick uncle in Hoboken. If it's wrong for Jenna's parents to lie, why was it all right for my father?

CHAPTER 32

I wouldn't let my father take Butch back before he could say goodbye to my animals. Betty put him in his cage and we took him out of the bathroom into my bedroom. Hammy was the first. I said, "Hammy, this is Butch, who's going away because we think he's sick. Would you like to say goodbye?"

Hammy was too busy running around on his wheel to pay attention. So we took Butch over to Oscar's tank. I said, "Oscar—wherever you are—" Because Oscar was hiding in his cave. I maybe saw him two minutes a day, and then he pretended not to know me. I said, "This is Butch. I know you don't care, but he's a sick bunny and I hope he's not dying."

And my goodness, Oscar swam out of his cave. He swam right past us—me, Butch, and Betty—though he didn't look at us once. Even so, I felt better for Butch. He had a chance to see Oscar. And I felt better for Oscar. He was a big, ugly fish, but maybe he wasn't so mean just because he ate Reddy. He came out to see

Butch, which he didn't have to. He had a heart.

Next we took Butch to say goodbye to Turtelini. Turtelini was on his rock, getting a tan from his heat lamp. I tapped on his window so he'd look at Butch, but I must have scared him. He dove off the rock into the water and swam into a corner and didn't once come out of his shell to say goodbye.

Of all my animals, Jessie said the best goodbye. Even though she was just a kitten and had never been in our house before, she behaved the nicest. First of all, I didn't even have to go looking for her, which was different from Timmy, who the minute we got home from Kate's and we let him out of his kennel, he disappeared. Who knows where? But Jessie stayed on my bed where I put her, and she didn't move until I came to get her to say goodbye to Butch. And when I put her on the floor in front of him in his cage, she went right up and stuck her tiny head almost between the bars, just to get a good look. And she looked and looked at Butch, who was lying there, not moving. And she stuck her paw inside the cage like she was waving to say goodbye. This was the kind of cat I wish Timmy was.

I called him over and over, "Timmy! Timmy!" hoping he was spying on us and could see what Jessie was doing and learn from her. It was hard to believe, but he never came out from wherever.

CHAPTER 33

The first day back at school, Mrs. Korman told us right after attendance that she had bad news about Butch. He got sick over vacation and the vet didn't know what was wrong. They were giving him tests, and she would let us know.

That night, in the middle of my Game Boy, Jenna called me. Mrs. Korman had just gotten off the phone with her mother. Butch had died. He had leukemia, which is a disease of the blood. Mrs. Korman called them because they were the ones supposed to be taking care of Butch during vacation. Jenna was crying when she told me. She said it was all my fault because Butch would have gotten better at our house because we were so good with animals. I agreed with her, so I started to cry. My mother heard me from all the way in her office and came to my room wanting to know why. When I told her, she got very calm in a way that makes me nervous and asked for the phone. She said, "Jenna, I'm sorry to hear about Butch. May I speak to your mother?"

When my mother gets calm that way, it's like every word that comes out of her mouth is as if she wrote it down first and was reading it. I mean, there's no way of talking back to her when she's that calm. You just know you're wrong and might as well go to jail.

I couldn't stand being in the room to hear her with Jenna's mother, so I went to the kitchen and poured a glass of one-percent milk, which calmed me down. I would have hung out in the kitchen until my mother got off the phone, but she called me back. She handed me the phone. Jenna was sobbing into it on the other end. "Julie, I'm sorry for what I said, I didn't mean it." She was crying hard. "I'm sorry, I'm sorry, I'm so sorry."

I started to cry. "I'm sorry, me too."

"I'm sorry," she said.

"Me too, I'm sorry."

The more times I said I'm sorry, the better I felt. By the time we got off the phone, I was still crying, but I actually felt pretty good.

The next morning I walked into the schoolyard, and first thing I saw Jenna. We dropped our book bags and rushed over to each other and hugged. When it was time to go in, we lined up together. We walked into school holding hands.

CHAPTER 34

From the first day, Jessie was easy to find, but as usual you never knew where to look for Timmy. I wanted them to be friends, but almost a week after we were home they hadn't even said hello. I don't know if they ever even saw each other. They were never in the same place. I'd pick Jessie up in my arms to take her where Timmy had been a second ago and he was gone.

I introduced Jessie to all my other animals. Oscar came right up to the front of the tank and stared at Jessie like, if we put her in, he'd try to eat her. Jessie was such a baby, I didn't think she even knew she was supposed to eat Oscar if she could. She didn't look interested.

She didn't look interested in eating Hammy either. If I took him out of his cage, I thought she might play with him, maybe they could be friends, the way she pawed at him. I wondered if I could try another Great Experiment. The thing was, Jessie looked so nearly human, like she might grow up into a person, not a cat. I mean, with a cat's head, but otherwise you couldn't tell her from anyone else. And she would never eat any of my pets.

My mother liked to watch her eat, she said she had table manners. If you had table manners, my mother liked you. Jessie was the only one of my pets she talked about. She bought her different-flavored cat food. Jessie only ate dry cat food, but my mother tried everything. She opened a can of tuna she uses to make me lunch to see what Jessie did with it. Our leftovers from dinner she put in her bowl.

But Jessie wasn't a big eater, she was a big drinker. She loved water, but not as much in a bowl. What she liked was to jump up on the sink and you had to turn on the faucet for her, and she drank water right as it poured out. It worried me that her head got soaked, but it didn't bother Jessie. When she was through drinking, she shook her head dry, spraying water all over me. It was fun. I'd come home after school and have to go to the bathroom, and Jessie was waiting for me in the sink like, Where were you, I've been here all day. Then she stared at me to turn on the faucet. I think she understood me talking to her. I know I understood her.

The end of my first week back at school, my mother called me into the kitchen after I got home. "Timmy and Jessie had a fight."

"No!"

"No one's hurt, but Timmy had a big scratch over

his eye. He's hiding, I don't know where."

"Where's Jessie?"

Just then Jessie walked into the kitchen, jumped up on the sink, and looked at me like, Well, why don't you turn on the water?

She looked a couple of inches bigger to me. "Jessie, you can have water, but you can't fight with Timmy. Okay?" I turned on the water. "I have to go find Timmy."

"I have more news," my mother said. She walked me out of the kitchen, with Jessie still drinking water from the sink. She walked me into my father's studio. On the floor was a big puddle of throw up. I said, "Timmy threw up again?"

My mother handed me a roll of paper towels. "Timmy didn't do it. This is Jessie's. She throws up after she drinks too much water. Don't let her drink too much. It's your job to clean it up."

"It's my job to go to school and do homework."

I had to say it, even though I knew it wasn't going to do me any good.

CHAPTER 35

Jessie threw up almost every day, some days twice. Before Betty went back home to Brazil, I could get her to clean it up. But after she left, it was my job. I hated it.

When we took Jessie in for her shots, the vet said it was probably hair balls and it wasn't serious. Jessie's shots made her sleepy. My father and I brought her home and put her on my bed and she didn't move, she just slept.

When I came back into my room after practicing the piano, which I don't like to do but they make me, Timmy was up on my bed too, sleeping next to Jessie, almost on top of her. I called everyone in to see.

My mother said, "Isn't that sweet!"

My father said, "Give them time and they'll get used to each other."

Halley said, "What are you talking about? Timmy's not even used to us."

CHAPTER 36

The day everything bad happened my mother picked me up after school. She was carrying flowers. "Who's coming to dinner?" I said. My mother likes flowers, but she usually forgets to buy them except for friends coming over. She laughed. "Actually, I got them for you, so we could dress up your room a little."

"What's wrong with my room?" I loved my room just the way it was.

"I love the zoo in your room, but I don't want you to forget there's a beautiful little girl living there too."

She showed me the flowers. There were a whole bunch of them wrapped tight in purple tissue paper. Lilies and roses and hyacinths was what she said they were. They smelled good and they were pretty, I guess, but I'm not that interested in flowers. I should have said thank you right away, except I was thinking of my new hermit crab I just got as a present. But my mother wasn't going to let me get away with that. She said sarcastically, "Thank you, Mommy."

Nobody in the history of the world loves good manners as much as my mother.

"Thank you, Mommy," I said. And I really didn't mind saying it. I just wish I had a day off from good manners sometime: "Thank you" and "You're welcome," "Excuse me" and "Please."

"Please" is a big deal with my mother. And you have to say it at the beginning of what you want, not at the end. She thinks it's rude if you say, "Pass the milk" and then go "Please," as if you just remembered that you're supposed to say it. The polite way is *"Please* pass the milk," or *"Will* you *please* pass the milk?"

No, that's wrong. *"Will* you" sounds too much like it's ordering you to pass the milk. *"Would* you please pass the milk?" is better because it's more like you're asking for a favor and they don't have to pass it if they don't want to. I mean, of course they'll pass the milk—why wouldn't they?—but my mother thinks they'll feel better if you ask nicely. Or they'll like you better. Something like that.

Anyway, I couldn't wait to get home from school to play with Hermy, this hermit crab that my cousin Glenn gave me a couple of weeks after Jessie came to live with us. Hermy lived inside his shell that he could move in and out of like it was a house. And what Glenn gave us to go with Hermy was a cage with two extra shells—one was red with blue stripes and the other was purple with yellow stripes. So Hermy could move out of one house into another anytime he felt like. Hermy didn't do much except eat seeds and berries and fruit, and drink water from a dish. From the minute I got him, he stayed inside the same shell he came in. He must have come out to eat when I was at school or asleep at night, because I only saw him do it once. I was dying to see him switch shells. That would have been a big deal for me. I said to him fifty or a hundred times, "Switch shells, Hermy," or "One, two, three, switch!" But he wouldn't do anything I told him.

Halley said, "You could get a rock for a pet and it would be more exciting."

Every day I waited to see him switch shells, but he must have been in the most comfortable shell in the world because he didn't switch like Glenn said he would. But Glenn also said all he knew about hermit crabs was what the man in the store told him. The man could have been lying just to get rid of those two extra shells.

My father was sure the man was lying. "I think Glenn has been caught in a shell game," he said. My mother laughed. If it was a joke, I didn't get it. Sometimes his jokes are too grown-up for me.

I had Hermy out of his tank on my bed with the two extra shells on both sides of him, practically holding my breath waiting for him to do something, when my mother came in and made me feel awful. She said, "I haven't seen you play with your hamster for a long time."

I couldn't believe how fast I got ashamed. I had paid so much attention to Jessie since she came, and to Hermy right after, that I hadn't paid any attention to my other pets. Oscar and Turtelini didn't care. And Timmy hid when I paid him attention. He paid attention to me only if I forgot about him, or pretended to. But Hammy adored the attention he got. Before we went away to Kate's, I took him out of his cage one or two times a day and put him on my bed, right where Hermy was that minute, and let him climb all over me from my belly to my nose and in and out of my hands, from my left hand to my right hand, and back and forth like that. He loved it! So did I.

But I hadn't had him out of his cage since I got Jessie. I just didn't have time. I mean, I fed him, I fed all my animals, and I made sure he had water. But it was true that I hadn't paid him much attention, and it was awful. What was even worse is, I didn't once think about it until my mother reminded me. I waited for my mother to leave the room because I couldn't stand her seeing how ashamed I was. Then I put Hermy away and ran to Hammy. I unhooked the door to his cage and reached in. He backed away. It was as if he didn't know me. But he had to know me. It was only a little more than a week, three or five days more. Not even.

I cried. Then I apologized. "I'm sorry, Hammy. I was bad. It's wrong what I did. I'm sorry, I'm sorry." He must have thought it over because after another second or two he came out of the corner he'd backed into and ran on top of my hand like the old days. I lifted him out of the cage and put him on my bed. Then I remembered my cats. I closed the door to my bedroom and the door to the bathroom and checked under the bed and in my closet. No Timmy or Jessie. I got on my bed ready to play with Hammy. And the bedroom door I just closed opened. My father walked in. "Julie, shouldn't you be doing your homework?"

"Close the door!" I shouted.

"Don't shout at me," my father said, but he closed the door. "I'll give you five more minutes with Hammy and then you have to do your homework." Then he said, "What happened here?" I mean, all of a sudden, like he just noticed something wrong.

I didn't know what he was talking about. I turned around and saw what he saw. Oscar's tank was green all over. The water looked wrong. It was dirty and slimy. When did that happen?

"When did this happen?"

I got scared because I didn't know, and my father sounded worried, so something was wrong.

"Is Oscar dead?"

"I'm sure he's okay. We'll find out." He took the top off Oscar's tank and started feeling around. "This water is slimy."

"Is Oscar dead?" I asked again.

"He can't last long in this slime. How long has it been like this?"

I looked at my father, so ashamed I couldn't stand it. First, I forgot about Hammy and now I had forgotten Oscar. What was wrong with me? I tried my hardest to make it not my fault. "It's not my fault!" I said to my father like I believed it. But I didn't, and he didn't either.

"Julie, we're going to empty this tank right now. You have to help me."

But how could I? I had Hammy in my hands, jumping from my right hand to my left hand and back. We hadn't played this game in so many days, I lost count. How could I get Hammy to trust me again and then shove him back in his cage before we played ten minutes? He'll *never* forgive me!

"Julie, *help!*" My father sounded annoyed because I wasn't helping. I could tell him why, but it was complicated, so I thought it was better to shut up. If I kept not doing anything, my father would fix Oscar all by himself even if he was mad at me. Anyhow, I didn't think he'd stay mad long. He never stayed mad long. He was like my mother that way.

I heard him say a bad word, then he started dumping rocks and plants out of the tank onto the floor. They made a mess. "I could use your help," he said, and then he said it again. "I could use your help, *please*." He put the "please" at the end, which wasn't polite. I didn't care about his bad manners, I was feeling awful because I was wrong no matter what I did. I decided that Hammy was the one I had to disappoint. He could only sulk when I put him away, he couldn't glare at me like my father.

My father picked up Oscar's tank. The plants and rocks and coral that belonged there were all over the floor of my room, making it wet and garbagy and disgusting. I wasn't going to say anything about it. The tank had to be heavy, full of this muddy green water. A ten-gallon tank. I don't know how heavy that is, but my father shouldn't have been carrying it, even to the bathroom, which was only the next room. "Open the bathroom door for me," he growled. He had a famous bad back in our family. I was worried he'd hurt himself. Sometimes his back went out and he had to sleep on the floor.

I was so worried for him, I forgot to open the door.

"Never mind," he said, like he couldn't stand me, and kicked the bathroom door open. He could hardly walk with the tank. He set it down on top of the toilet, balancing it there. He felt around inside. How could he put his hand in that yuck? "Where is that fish?" he yelled at me, like I was supposed to tell him.

It was impossible to find Oscar in all that slime.

He caught a deep breath and picked up the tank, which it hurt to watch him lift. He turned it over into the sink. The mess it made, you have never seen such a mess! My mother would kill him. The slimy water in the sink went round and round, down the drain, leaving black glop on the sides. He poured out the last of the water and it slopped over the sink, then out came Oscar in a green and brown and black splash so awful I wanted to run. But I couldn't desert my father. Oscar jumped in the air. He didn't want to be in that sink, who could blame him? My father smacked him on his head with a slap. Oscar fell back into the sink. "I hate this!" my father yelled.

Oscar jumped out of the sink again, and my father slapped him back. I could see what my father hated most was the idea of Oscar falling on the floor and he'd have to pick him up with his bare hands. I didn't know why that would bother him—his hands were already in all that slime. But my father doesn't like fish any more than my mother. Maybe to eat, okay, but he never went fishing, not once in his life.

Oscar jumped up in the air three or four or five times. He looked like he was going for the ceiling. My father yelled, "I don't know what to do, I don't know

what to do!" He sounded like he was ready to cry. He looked away from Oscar. "Go get your mother!"

And because he was looking away for a second, my father slapped late at Oscar's last jump and he missed. Oscar flew past his hand, out of the sink and into the toilet, landing with a splash.

I screamed, "Don't flush!"

My father fell on the floor laughing. "Don't flush!" he said over and over, as if I said the funniest joke he ever heard in his life.

"Julie, quick, bring me the top of Oscar's tank," he said, choking and laughing. I brought it extra fast so my father would have to forgive me for all my mistakes. And with only one hand. I held on to Hammy with my other. My father covered the open toilet with the top of Oscar's tank. Now Oscar wouldn't be able to jump out onto the bathroom floor. "Why didn't you just put the toilet seat down?" I asked him.

"Would you want me to put the toilet seat down on Oscar?"

I didn't want to think about it. I said, "I'll go get Mom."

"Wait," my father said. "I don't want her to see what I've done to the bedroom and bathroom. Let's clean up a little." My father lifted the empty tank. "What a relief, it's so light." He bent over to put the tank into the bathtub. I don't know what happened next. I saw the tank drop out of my father's hands when he had it most of the way into the tub. He fell back. His shoulder hit the sink. He screamed. I screamed. My father was on the floor, all bent in a twisty way. One leg was hanging over the tub. The

tank was inside the tub lying on the rubber shower mat where he dropped it. It hadn't broken. My father was breathing very hard and groaning the S word a lot. "Are you okay?" I said. What a stupid thing to say.

My father's face was white, his head was on the floor looking at me with his eyes squinched and his teeth clenched. He had his right leg on the bathroom floor and his left leg hanging over the tub. "It's only my back." He smiled at me. "I'm fine." He wanted me to be calm. But he was my father, twisted on the floor in lots of pain. What was I supposed to do?

"Julie, lift my leg off the tub. Put it on the floor."

I'm only a kid. How could I touch him, I was so scared.

"It's okay," he said. I wished he'd stop smiling. It made me feel the opposite of what he wanted me to feel. I took his left leg and lifted it off the tub very, very gently, like it was a baby. He groaned, which made me almost drop it, but he said in the middle of the groan, "Good. You're doing great." I got the leg on the floor. It was stiff and bent. The other was lying flat.

"Does it hurt?" I asked him. I could only say stupid things.

"It's only my back. You've seen this before."

No, I hadn't. I'd seen him in bed with a bad back before. I never saw him fall over in the bathroom before.

"Get your mother."

I started to go. Then he said, "Better put Hammy away."

Hammy! Where was Hammy? When my father fell, I must have let Hammy go. But where? *"Hammy!"* I yelled.

"Get your mother." My father was talking in a whisper, reminding me I should help him before I looked for Hammy.

I ran out of the bathroom, hoping I'd see Hammy on the bed or somewhere, but I couldn't stop to look even if I wanted. I stopped, though, to open my door very carefully and just enough so Hammy couldn't escape. Or if he tried to squeeze through, I could catch him. Also, so that Timmy and Jessie couldn't get in, or if they tried I could chase them away.

I closed the door really fast behind me. I saw my mother down the hall, coming out of the kitchen. She was carrying this beautiful vase, her favorite, white and sparkly like ice melting. And in it the flowers she bought for my room squeezed so tight they looked like a jungle. Her face was that special face she had only when she did something she was proud of for the house.

And then she saw me running at her and her face all changed. Her eyes got wide, her mouth went open. Before, she was walking slow and kind of dancy, as if every step was fun. One look at me and she started to run. "What's wrong?" she shouted. She ran past the hall table that stands just outside our living room.

"Daddy! Daddy in the bathroom!"

She didn't stop running. She almost threw the vase of flowers at me. It would have crashed on the floor in a million pieces if I hadn't grabbed it. I almost let it drop.

I held it tight, it was her favorite. I didn't want any more mistakes.

My mother was opening the door to my bedroom. "He's not dead!" I yelled, because I was afraid I scared her more than I meant to. She screamed and ran into my bedroom, leaving the door wide open.

"Shut the door!" I started to run, but I couldn't. I had this big ugly thing full of flowers I didn't want that my mother was making me put in my room.

I looked around for where I could get rid of the vase, so I could run and close my bedroom door. The hall table was closest, covered by a big shawl and piles of show-offy books that I never saw my mother and father open a single one of. That's where I put the vase, just as I saw Timmy and Jessie on their way out of the living room. Jessie was in front, Timmy was a little bit behind. I could see they were looking at the open bedroom door. I yelled as loud as I could, "Timmy and Jessie!" They stopped just long enough for me to catch up with them. I made every scary noise I knew how to make. Timmy backed away, but Jessie I couldn't scare.

I had to yell at her six times or more before she looked at me like, "What's your problem?" and walked back into the living room.

I ran back into my bedroom and slammed the door shut. In the bathroom, I heard my mother saying, "You'll be fine. Easy. Easy. You'll be fine." My father was using words I'm not allowed to hear. When I got to them, my mother was holding my father halfway up. He looked like he could fall down on top of her any second. She moved him out the door so carefully, it was like she was carrying the vase I almost just dropped.

The door she moved him out of was to their bedroom. We have two doors to that bathroom, one to their room, one to mine. I heard squishy-flapping sounds and I knew just where to look. There was Oscar in the toilet bowl trying to jump out, banging his big head against the top of the tank my father covered the toilet with, then falling back in.

I needed to help. I leaned over into the bathtub and turned on the faucets and started pouring water into Oscar's tank. I was going to actually clean Oscar's tank all by myself. My father would be so amazed, he'd faint.

I heard him groan from the bedroom. I ran out to see. My mother had him sitting on the edge of their bed. He couldn't lie down and he couldn't stand up, he was just sort of frozen stiff, leaning over, like he wanted to tie his shoelace.

My mother said, "What can I get you?" He said at the exact same time, "I'm fine." They mustn't have heard each other, because they kept saying the same thing at the same time over and over. My mother looked helpless. My father looked miserable. It scared me to look at them.

"Hi, Hammy," my father said. He was looking down at his feet, so I did too. Hammy was inside his sneaker that my mother had taken off him.

"Julie, turn off the bathroom water before it overflows!" my mother said. But I reached out to get Hammy.

"Now, Julie. Hammy is fine." She had her I-better-do-what-she-says look. I didn't care. I grabbed my father's sneaker and ran into the bathroom. I turned off the tub water, which wasn't even halfway up to the top.

That took only a second, but when I looked back at my father's sneaker, Hammy wasn't in it anymore. I ran back into my parents' bedroom. "Is he in here?" I yelled. My mother was trying, one inch at a time, to get my father into bed. They weren't about to worry about Hammy.

I ran back through the bathroom, past Oscar in the toilet—"Hi, Oscar!"—into my bedroom. I was just about to look under my bed for Hammy when he ran out, right toward me. I had him!

Except Halley opened my door. "What's going on here? I'm trying to do my homework!"

"No!" I screamed. Timmy and Jessie rushed in like

they couldn't wait another second. Hammy practically ran into them, then he saw his mistake. He turned and ran under the bed. I put out my leg, trying to block Timmy and Jessie, but I only had one leg for two cats. I screamed at them, "No, Jessie! No, Timmy!"

I fell on my knees, on my way under the bed, at the exact second Jessie ran out past me. She had Hammy. My Hammy was in her mouth. He was alive but in her mouth. Timmy ran out from under the bed and ran

right into me. He looked up at me for a second like he wanted to ask, "Which way did they go?"

Both me and Halley ran out in the hall after Jessie, who scooted under the hall table with Hammy. I couldn't see them under there. There was this shawl that covered the table that blocked my seeing under it. I grabbed the shawl. I meant to lift it aside so I could get at Jessie and make her drop Hammy. I didn't remember there was a vase full of flowers and a hundred books on top. I must have pulled too hard, it was like the whole world went flying up into the air.

The vase with the flowers my mother bought for my room made the loudest crash I ever heard. My mother's favorite vase. The books went flying, flowers and pieces of flowers and pieces of vase going smash all over the hall rug. The noise scared Jessie. It was enough to make her run out from under the table, but not enough to drop Hammy. Halley yelled at the top of her lungs, "No, Jessie!"

But that only made her run harder, with Hammy in her mouth, right into the kitchen. Halley ran after her. I couldn't run, I was too scared to try. I was slipping and sliding in the middle of the books and flowers and thousands of pieces of broken vase on the floor.

"There she goes!" I heard Halley yell. Jessie ran out of the kitchen. Hammy was still alive and wiggling in her mouth, but only a little, like she was afraid of making a fuss. As if it was a jailbreak, Jessie zipped past me, back to my room. Halley was out of the kitchen after her, coming right at me. She stopped all of a sudden and went all white. Her hands grabbed her face. I don't know why, but she screamed: "Oh my god, oh my god, oh my god!"

Was Hammy dead? Jessie must have eaten Hammy. My mother ran out from helping my father, and took one look at me, and *she* started screaming. "Oh my god, Julie, oh my god. Julie, Julie, Julie!"

Julie what? I didn't do anything. I wasn't anywhere near Jessie. I didn't know why they were screaming. I mean, they were really upset. I began to think it wasn't about Jessie, it was about me. But what about me? I looked where they were looking, which was down at my leg, my right leg. And on the inside of my thigh, where my pants used to be, it was ripped open and a huge flap of skin—my skin!—was hanging loose like a piece of salami. Hanging like that and bleeding. Not a lot. But a little is more than I really needed to know about. I started screaming. All three of us were screaming. My mother's vase when it broke had cut open my thigh.

I stopped worrying about Hammy in Jessie's mouth. I worried instead that something wasn't normal with me. And if my mother was so scared and Halley too— what was happening? Was I going to die?

All of us weren't screaming anymore, we were crying.

I heard my father from the bedroom yell, "Is anything wrong?" I didn't understand how this amazing thing could happen to me when this was supposed to be about saving Hammy, not a flap of my skin that made me want to throw up looking at it.

CHAPTER 37

After the first minute or so, when it was the worst I felt, none of it was actually that bad. I mean, very fast it became normal. Scary but normal. More like TV. I knew everything that was going on, but it wasn't real. It hurt a little, but not that much. It might as well be happening to someone else.

Everyone took turns being calm after the screaming. But no one was more calm than me. For example, when my mother said we had to go to the hospital, I couldn't believe she was making so much fuss over a cut. How about we just put on a Band-Aid? My father said he wasn't going to let me go to the hospital without him. My mother said, "You're insane, you can't stand up." My father said, "I'm going." My mother said, "How are you going?" My father said, "I'll get there." I mean, they sounded just like their regular selves to me, this was how they talked even when I wasn't cut.

My mother and Halley, both of them holding on to me tight, got me down to the lobby. But we couldn't call a cab because we had to wait for my father, who could hardly walk and wouldn't let anyone do anything for him. At first, Halley wanted to help him get dressed and out so it wouldn't take so long. But he didn't want that. He said, "Go with Julie, she needs you." And then, all by himself, he started to put his pants and shoes on. And after he made us go, he had to get himself all the way out of the bedroom to the front door and into the hall and down in the elevator. I made my mother and Halley wait for him in the lobby because I wasn't going to the hospital without him. Anyway, I knew he was coming, I could hear him groaning all the way down in the elevator.

Orlando, the doorman, got us a cab. But with my father it was going to take ten minutes to fit him in the backseat, and if he was stretched out the way he had to be, nobody else could sit in the back. So my mother said to Halley, "I'll take Julie. You and Daddy meet us in the emergency room."

CHAPTER 38

My mother took me to Roosevelt Hospital. This was the middle of the night. Actually, it wasn't, it couldn't have been, but it felt like it. Everybody was there, it was like everyone sick in the city decided to go there that day. That part was interesting.

My mother asked me too many times, was I all right? I was fine, I just wanted this to be over with so I could go home. None of this was my idea. And it took way, way too long before Halley and my father showed up in the emergency room. So the true answer to my mother asking me, "Are you all right?" was "No, not until Daddy and Halley are here." I wanted my father and sister with me, then they could cut off my leg for all I cared. Not really. I wondered if they would cut my leg off. I didn't think so.

Finally, maybe after a half hour, they got there. My father, the way he looked, was worse off than the other patients in the emergency room, and he wasn't actually a patient, I was. He was bent in half. But it didn't stop him from making jokes. It's not so funny hearing jokes from your father who's bent like a pretzel, especially if you're in a hospital to have them cut your leg off.

But the nurses were nice. We waited over two and a half hours before they were ready for me. I was the only kid there my age, though they usually had lots of kids, one of the nurses told me. Another nurse gave me soda and candy. In the entire two and a half hours, all the nurses came over and talked to me. Nobody wanted to talk to my father, who was stretched out on the floor by now. He was flat on his back so he wouldn't hurt. And all around him, on every side, there were people in pain—real patients—sitting or standing, so it embarrassed me that my father, who wasn't even there to see a doctor, they let lie on the floor.

It took nineteen stitches to sew me up. This big flap of skin inside my right thigh. Because of the shot they gave me, it didn't hurt. I didn't feel anything. And there wasn't that much blood. It was amazing. It wasn't a doctor who sewed me but a nurse that they call a nurse practitioner. She does everything a doctor does, but better. Even so you call her nurse. Her name was Miss Price. She was more like a fairy godmother, nice and gentle. Older than my mother and father, with short gray hair like a soldier. I thought she was beautiful. Miss Price asked me about the zoo in my room and what I fed my animals, and hoped I was wrong that Hammy was dead, but if he was I should forgive Jessie because it's natural for cats to eat hamsters, so it's not their fault if they catch them outside of a cage, it's not anybody's, accidents happen, look what happened to me.

Miss Price gave me so much to think about I forgot, almost, that she was sticking this needle in me, sewing on this patch, except it wasn't a patch, it was my own skin that she was putting back in place where it was supposed to be, with a needle and nineteen stitches.

I wouldn't have minded, except for my family. My father on the floor yelling, "How you doing, sweetie? I know you're doing great," my mother holding my hand so tight I thought she thought I was going to die. "You're so brave, isn't she brave? Isn't she the bravest child you've ever seen?"

And forget about Halley! I've never been so embarrassed. I'm proud she loved me so much, but I couldn't stand how upset she was. She kept telling me how sorry she was, when she didn't do anything. "Let them cut me, not you, I wish I could bleed for you! I wish I could have two hundred cuts so you don't have to have one!"

Fine. But really.

The last ten stitches I made myself watch Miss Price sew up. My mother and Halley couldn't look. It's harder to look if it's not you. If it's you, it's kind of—I don't know what it is, I just needed to know. I'd be mad at myself for missing it, if I wondered later. While Miss Price was putting in the stitches, I was thinking, This isn't happening to me, yes it is, no it isn't.

Later, my mother was crying and telling me I was so brave. And my father, who half the emergency room helped put back on his feet, had tears in his eyes, and *he* was telling me how brave I was. And Halley was teary, hugging and kissing me. "Julie, you're my hero." I was embarrassed, them treating me that way. It wasn't me who did anything. I just sat there and got sewed up.

Outside the hospital, three hours after this stupid thing happened, I sat in a wheelchair while my mother waved at cabs. One for me and her, one for my father and Halley. For two or three minutes, nobody paid attention to me so it was my first chance to think.

CHAPTER 39

I thought about Hammy.

Going home in the cab, I thought, Maybe he got away. Maybe when we got home, Hammy and Jessie and Timmy would be playing with each other. Just like in the Great Experiment. I didn't want to believe Hammy was dead. I wasn't mad at Jessie. I loved Jessie. Eating hamsters and mice and gerbils and guinea pigs is what cats do. It's their job. Miss Price said so.

I wanted to be sadder than I was, but I was tired. My mother said I was in shock. Shock left me feeling pheh, so I couldn't be sad about Hammy the way I thought I deserved. I was so tired I wanted to wake up tomorrow morning in bed and the first thing, when I opened my eyes, I'd see Hammy running around in his cage.

I didn't think it was going to happen unless I fell asleep in the cab. My mother put an arm tight around me and hugged me. She hugged me until I fell asleep, and it was in the cab just like I wanted. It was the only good thing that happened that day.

CHAPTER 40

The house was spooky quiet. The hall was disgusting, with flowers and pieces of vase and books everywhere. And the shawl that made me get my cut and got my hamster killed was a mess on the floor, soaking wet from the water that splashed all over when the vase broke. I hated that shawl. I wanted my mother to throw it out, or give it away to a homeless person. But come to think of it, I didn't want that either. The shawl had a curse on it, the homeless person would get sick and die. My mother should throw it in the garbage. Where it belonged. Even garbage was too good for it.

I didn't see dead Hammy anywhere I looked, though I didn't look that hard. My bedroom door was wide open. I walked over the mess in the hall, a little scared to go in. But it was all right, Hammy wasn't dead there either. And who did I find on my bed, as if they didn't do anything? Fast asleep. Like nothing happened. Timmy and Jessie lying next to each other.

"I refuse to sleep in this bed tonight!" I said, with no

one there to hear me. I looked under the bed for Hammy's body. I couldn't help myself. It was dark. I didn't see Hammy. Was he inside Jessie? In her tummy, asleep on my bed? I didn't know if I could ever sleep in that bed again.

I looked at my bandage in the full-size mirror on the closet door. It was huge. It went from the top of my leg almost down to my knee. But I didn't hurt. Miss Price said it would be four weeks before the stitches came out, then we'd see. Would I have a scar all the way down? How ugly would that be? Some scars could be neat, the way tattoos are. Tattoos are only scars made up to look like they're designs. If I didn't like my scar, maybe I could turn it into a tattoo.

I heard a splash in the bathroom and I thought someone was using the toilet. Then I remembered: Oscar! I ran into the bathroom. There he was, not even trying to get out, just swimming round and round like the toilet was his swimming pool. But he was swimming slower than I wanted him to. He didn't look good. I couldn't have him die on me. Not him *and* Hammy.

I started to call my father but remembered he couldn't move. So how could he bend over to clean out Oscar's tank in the bathtub, and fill it for me, and carry it full of water into my room? I went to find Halley. She was on her cell phone in her room talking to her friend Desiree about my adventure. The way Halley tells a story, you can see it happening, like a movie. It was a funny story the way she told it—even the part about Hammy and my father's back. But not my cut, she didn't make that funny. I would have been mad at her if she tried to make my cut funny.

I was scared to ask her to help me with the fish tank. She didn't like fish. She was like my parents that way— she thought fish were disgusting. So I was sure she wouldn't help, then what was I supposed to do? If I didn't have shock, I would have cried.

Halley said *yes*! I couldn't believe it. I have such a great sister! "I'll only help if I can do the decoration," she said, walking me fast into the bathroom. I hadn't thought about decoration. All I wanted was to get some water in the tank, so Oscar and Hammy wouldn't die on the same day. But Halley was right—there was this extra junk to put in, most of it lying on my bedroom floor. Rocks and pebbles and coral and plants that Oscar had mostly eaten. Stuff like that, all lying where my father dumped it, this wet, slimy gunk all over my floor. I didn't want to touch it. Let Halley decorate! *Goody!*

We lifted the tank out of the tub and carried it into my bedroom. We put it down on top of my dresser, because it needed to go somewhere and we couldn't get it back up on the bookshelf by ourselves. Halley went to work on the tank, and I went to see how Oscar was doing. Not good. I had to get him out of the toilet fast. I thought I could maybe lean over and pick him up out of the toilet bowl with my hands and drop him in the sink and fill the sink with fresh water for him to swim in. But I couldn't stand the idea. Putting my bare hands in the toilet bowl to pick up a live, dying fish? I went to find my mother.

She was in the hall, cleaning up the vase I broke. She looked sad. "This was one of my favorites," she said. At least she wasn't blaming me. I said, "We have to get Oscar out of the toilet."

"Ask your father."

"He can't bend."

She made a face that showed me how much she didn't want to help. "Do you have a net?"

"I don't know where it is."

She made another face, worse than the first one. "How are we supposed to get Oscar out of the toilet without a net?"

"He's going to die in there," I said.

My mother went into the kitchen, I hoped it wasn't to wash the dishes. When she had a problem she didn't like, she made the problem wait and washed dishes. She came out of the kitchen. She was carrying a strainer—one of those wire things you dump spaghetti in to get rid of the water you cook it in. We walked toward my bedroom. I didn't say anything, she didn't say anything. She looked at the two cats asleep on my bed and said, "Are they for real?" She didn't sound happy.

I followed her into the bathroom. She handed me the strainer. "Okay," she said.

I looked at Oscar in the toilet. Poor Oscar. I couldn't do it. I handed the strainer back to my mother.

"Halley!" my mother yelled.

Halley didn't answer. We went back into the bedroom, me and my mother. Halley must have come in just after us. She was decorating Oscar's tank. She had wiped up all the yicky stuff on the floor with paper towels and was designing a whole new home for Oscar in the tank. If he lived. Which I was scared he wouldn't.

"I'm building a little fence here of pebbles and rocks and right here I'm putting a cave, a deep, deep cave. And on the opposite side, see, I'm putting in these plants. And these bigger rocks I'm turning into a second cave, so now he'll have a shallow cave and a deep cave." She was excited, waving her hands around a lot, the way she does when she's happy. Making a home for my fish made her happy. And she hated fish.

"I want to see!" my father yelled from his bed.

"You can't see because your back went out at the worst time for everyone!" my mother yelled back at him.

"Thank you!" my father yelled back at her. He sounded sarcastic.

My mother handed Halley the strainer. "You're doing

a beautiful job. You can finish after you get Oscar out of the toilet."

Halley gave my mother this look that would have scared anyone else except my mother. "Wha-a-a-a-t?" She made "what" sound like the longest word you ever heard, like it had twenty syllables.

My mother stared at her, then stared at me. "Halley's right. You're both right. You've just had nineteen stitches." She picked up the strainer from where Halley had dropped it on the floor and carried it into the bathroom.

Halley handed me a bucket and the two of us took turns going back and forth from my room to the bathtub, filling Oscar's tank with water. We must have gone in and out of the bathroom fifteen times, filling this ten-gallon tank. And every time we walked in and walked out, we had to pass my mother looking down into the toilet, holding the strainer out in her two hands but not moving an inch. She looked paralyzed.

"We're ready!" Halley yelled to my mother from the bedroom when the tank was full. It looked a lot better than it did when my father decorated it. All it needed now was the filter to be attached, but my father was going to have to clean it first, maybe tomorrow when he could stand again, if Oscar wasn't dead.

I left Halley to go back into the bathroom to watch my mother. I was sure she was going to do it even if she hated it. She wasn't going to let Oscar die. I think Oscar floating dead in the toilet felt worse to her than her hating to stick the strainer in the toilet. Suddenly she swooped. Water splashed every which way out of the bowl. She stood up straight and came at me with her eyes closed. She couldn't look. "Do I have him?"

I looked. "You've got him!"

My mother ran into the bedroom, her eyes squinty enough so she could just see where she was going but not Oscar flapping in the strainer. He was weak, he wasn't trying to get out. Halley and I jumped out of her way. With her eyes squinted shut, my mother turned the strainer over into the tank. Oscar fell out. He just lay there. On top of the water, looking like a dead gangster.

I didn't want him to be dead. I cheered at him, Halley too. "Swim, Oscar, swim, Oscar!" Maybe he heard. Suddenly he dived down to the bottom of the

174

tank, gobbled up a whole bunch of food flakes Halley had put in, then took off, back and forth across the tank exactly like the old Oscar, before the toilet bowl.

My mother had tears in her eyes. Halley and I grabbed her and hugged her. "Wait here while I throw this strainer in the garbage," she said.

My father yelled from the bedroom, "Is he okay? Somebody come in here and tell me what's happening!" We started into the bedroom when my mother, halfway back to the kitchen, stopped us by yelling, "The cats!" Halley spun around and ran into the bathroom. She grabbed the cover of the fish tank off the floor and jumped practically into my bedroom. She slammed it down on top of the tank and put a hand over her heart. We caught our breath. We began to giggle. Then we remembered to look over at my bed. Timmy and Jessie were fast asleep.

We went in to tell my father what happened.

CHAPTER 41

Every day of his bad back, my father got crankier. When he starts out, his backaches put him in a good mood, I don't know why. He jokes, he laughs, he thanks everybody a hundred times for doing practically nothing, like bringing him a snack in bed. But the longer he can't walk, the more he thinks he's better when he isn't, and he gets up like he's normal and sometimes even gets as far as the kitchen. Then you hear a loud "Ouch!" and my mother has to help him back to bed. A day that starts like that, you don't want to go near him.

It took four whole days for him to be able to stand up and walk where he didn't have pain so he could go out and do things. Before he got cranky, the first thing he promised when he could go out was he'd buy me a new hamster. But after he promised and I talked a lot about it, I decided a hamster was going to remind me too much of Hammy. I was already reminded every time I looked at Jessie. I thought of Hammy inside her tummy. I tried to think of him still in one piece, sleeping inside Jessie's tummy. That was all right, kind of.

I wanted a pet something like Hammy, but not too much. So I thought about what that could be, and asked my father to get me a gerbil. He said yes because he wasn't cranky anymore.

That night, thinking about it in my tent, I got nervous that a gerbil might not be a good idea because it was too close to a hamster. I was sleeping in my tent on my bedroom floor ever since we came home from the hospital. It's a plastic, kind of squeezed-together tent that pops out when you open it and want to use it. I play with it a lot when I remember to, and ever since Jessie ate Hammy and she started sleeping on my bed, I wasn't going near my bed.

So my mother got my pop-up tent out of the closet, and she unhooked it, and it popped and all I had to do (my mother actually did it) was put a sleeping bag on top of a thick pile of blankets inside the tent. And I had a bed that was just as comfortable and more fun than the bed I didn't want to go near with Jessie and Timmy sleeping on it.

So I was inside my tent and I started to wonder what I could get that was adorable like Hammy but different enough so I wouldn't be sad. I bet I wouldn't be so reminded of Hammy if I had *two* gerbils who would be with each other all the time, and would never be alone. (Hammy was always alone.) One gerbil by himself would be way too much like Hammy. But two? I'd look at them and think it's a whole different adventure.

My father was on his feet again so it was a good time to ask him about it. His back looked straight—well, it was never actually straight, he always stooped a little, but he was straighter than in a long time. So he was in such a good mood, I could have asked for three gerbils and gotten away with it.

He told me maybe I should start thinking of names for my gerbils before we went to the pet shop later. But I already had names, I just wasn't ready to tell him. I was afraid he'd laugh at me. I was positive Halley would. So I was keeping the names to myself for a while. Hammy and Hamsty were the names of my new gerbils.

You'd think that would remind me, but the two names lumped together, Hammy and Hamsty. I mean, I couldn't say one without thinking of the other. Maybe in the beginning I might be reminded. A little. But after I got used to it, I know I wouldn't.

I get lots of good ideas like that.

CHAPTER 42

My mother, at the last minute, decided to come with us
to the pet shop to buy the gerbils. "Can Halley go?" I
asked. I loved Halley to come to the pet shop with me.
But my mother said Halley had gone out, she didn't
know where. She smiled at my father, who didn't even
look at her, as if he was thinking of something else,
maybe his back. "Let's go," he said.

We got on the elevator. My mother was making
jokes all the way down, like she hadn't since she got
Oscar out of the toilet with her strainer and she had to
throw it away and her favorite vase broke.

We got downstairs. The elevator door opened on the
lobby. The first thing I saw, the second the door
opened, was six Chihuahua puppies and a tall, brown
lady who was pulling them back on their leashes to stop
them from jumping up and down on me.

They were yapping like crazy and trying to get into
the elevator with us, so we almost couldn't get off. The
lady kept pulling them back. She didn't live in our

building, she had to be visiting someone. I was jealous of who. I wished it was me.

Halley was in the lobby, standing a little behind the lady. She had the biggest grin I ever saw. Her fists were going up and down in the air as if she was a cheerleader or something. Why was she so excited?

My mother said, "Julie, this is Liz. Say hello and shake hands." Okay, my mother is big on manners, but why now? I wanted to play with the puppies. I could shake hands later.

My mother said, "Liz is a breeder. She breeds Chihuahuas. She has a kennel on Long Island. We asked her to come here today to show you some of her nicest puppies."

My father said, "Julie, any puppy you pick is yours."

My mother said, "Because you are the bravest girl we ever saw in our lives."

I was confused even before I was happy. "But I can't have a dog until I'm ten and a half." I was afraid that when they remembered the rules they'd change their minds.

"*Today* you're ten and a half. I'm making it official," my father said. "Happy birthday!"

"You've proved that you're the right age to take care of a dog," my mother said. "Absolutely the right age."

I was on my knees in the middle of these brown, jumpy, squirming, huffing and puffing beautiful puppies. One of them was going to be mine! And they were licking and leaping and pawing at me. This one—no, this one—that one—no, this—no—

I wanted Liz to decide for me. "I can't decide," I told her. I almost wanted to cry, but I knew how dumb that was.

Liz was the calmest person in the lobby. My mother and father and Halley were hysterical. Orlando the doorman couldn't stop grinning. Liz was the only one who knew what to do. "Go down to the other end of the lobby, Julie," she said. "Call your dog. Make up a name and call your dog."

"What if they all come?"

"I'll kill myself if they all come," my father said. He was joking.

"I don't think they'll all come," Liz said. "They don't know you. They are still very attached to me. I think only one or two will come, and then won't it be easier to make your pick?"

All I could think of was problems. "But I don't have a name," I said.

"You're good at names," my father said.

"You'll think of one," my mother said.

I walked to the other end of the lobby. My heart was beating a mile a minute. I wanted to scream. What if none of them came? What if the wrong one came? They were all so adorable, I wanted to keep them all. But actually I didn't. It was too much to take care of six puppies. Anyhow, I kind of had a favorite, but I was sure he wouldn't come. Or was he a she? I didn't care.

This wasn't supposed to happen until I was older. But it was happening today. And there was one reason why. And when I thought of that reason, I thought of the name.

I got down on my knees at the other end of the lobby. "Okay," I said to Liz. She dropped the leashes. I watched the Chihuahuas run around her and in and out between her legs. They loved Liz. They paid no attention to my mother or father or Halley. They had forgotten me.

It didn't matter. Just that second, I knew who'd

come when I called. I yelled out from my end of the lobby, "Stitches! Come, Stitches! Here, Stitches!"

My parents and Halley looked at each other and laughed out loud.

Stitches came running.